"Are you only being nice to me because you think you owe it to my family?"

Elsie's blunt comment took him off guard. "I... At first that was the reason."

"And now?"

Wariness darkened her eyes, but desire also flickered in the depths. Deke didn't quite know how to answer.

"Now..." He hesitated, hating the churning in his stomach. "Now I want to protect you."

Disappointment tightened her mouth. "Because you think I'm helpless? Well, I'm not, Deke. I know how to fight, how to take care of myself, how to shoot that gun. And I won't hesitate to do it."

"That doesn't mean you have to face everything alone all the time, Elsie."

Emotions clouded her eyes. "I don't know any other way."

He twined her fingers in his own, stroking her palm with his other hand as he pulled her into his lap. "Let me show you."

RITA HERRON

RETURN TO FALCON RIDGE

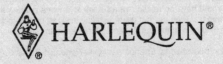

HARLEQUIN®

TORONTO • NEW YORK • LONDON
AMSTERDAM • PARIS • SYDNEY • HAMBURG
STOCKHOLM • ATHENS • TOKYO • MILAN • MADRID
PRAGUE • WARSAW • BUDAPEST • AUCKLAND

To all those fans who read *The Man from Falcon Ridge*
and asked for Elsie's story—hope you enjoy!

And to Jenny Bent for loving the dark, creepy stuff!

ISBN 0-373-88692-6

RETURN TO FALCON RIDGE

ABOUT THE AUTHOR

Award-winning author Rita Herron wrote her first book when she was twelve, but didn't think real people grew up to be writers. Now she writes so she doesn't have to get a *real* job. A former kindergarten teacher and workshop leader, she traded her storytelling for kids for romance, and writes romantic comedies and romantic suspense. She lives in Georgia with her own romantic hero and three kids. She loves to hear from readers, so please write her at P.O. Box 921225, Norcross, GA 30092-1225, or visit her Web site at www.ritaherron.com.

Books by Rita Herron

CAST OF CHARACTERS

Deke Falcon—A tough P.I. with a soft spot for wounded birds of prey—and women in trouble.

Elsie Timmons—She disappeared twenty years ago. But now that she's returned to Wildcat, Tennessee, someone wants her dead.

Howard Hodges—Just the thought of the man gives Elsie nightmares. Will the vile acts he committed against the girls at Wildcat Manor be exposed?

Hattie Mae Hodges—Did she die of natural causes, or was she murdered to stop her from telling the truth about what happened at Wildcat Manor?

Sheriff Andy Bush—He vowed to protect the citizens of Wildcat—but he wants Elsie run out of town at any cost.

Dr. Morty Mires—He provided health care for the pregnant teens housed at Wildcat Manor. But what is he hiding?

Burt Thompson—How far will he go to keep Elsie from digging up the past?

Renee Leberman—The social worker who helped arrange the adoptions for the pregnant teens died suddenly. What secrets did she take to her grave?

Eleanor Cross & Donna Burgess—They both adopted babies from teens at the orphanage, and will do anything to stop Elsie from exposing the adoptions.

Prologue

She was going to die in Wildcat Manor.

Fourteen-year-old Elsie Timmons shivered as the lock turned on the door, sealing the girls into their dismal cavern. The orphanage was haunted.

At night, the cries and screams taunted her. But they were her punishment.

And this was where she belonged. In the town of the damned where wildcats as big as tigers roamed the woods. Where the unwanted were hidden away forever. Where children disappeared into the forest, possibly eaten by the monsters.

Because they were all evil.

Elsie had known she was ever since she was four. Ever since she'd told her mama that the man next door was hurting her friend Hailey. Then Hailey and her family had been butchered, and her daddy had dragged her off, claiming they'd come for her next. Either the killer or the law.

Because she had brought the evil upon Hailey and her family.

Tears filled her eyes and dribbled down her cheeks. She wanted to change, but then she'd failed, and Daddy had left her here, alone, trapped in the tangled lies of Wildcat Manor.

Her hand went to her stomach. The images of the dark basement where she'd been taken last week still tormented her dreams. The sounds of her own cries. The sounds of others. The gripping pain that she had barely survived.

The emptiness that now consumed her.

Trees rattled and shook their winter fury against the thin, fog-coated glass panes, shrouding any light from the outside. Heavy footsteps shuffled down the corridor outside her room, and she hunched over in the shadows of the wall behind her bed, hoping to be invisible.

Little Torrie huddled beneath the faded quilts covering her cot, a low whimper of fear drifting toward her. Elsie was big and could take care of herself. She had been doing it for ages.

Torrie was nothing but a child, only eleven, with long blond hair and the eyes of an angel. Surely, *he* wouldn't hurt her….

Suddenly a key rattled in the door, and the ancient stone walls throbbed with the sound of the door screeching open. Elsie held her breath as he entered. The vile smell of whiskey floated into the musty space, and evil kissed her neck as he shuffled forward in the darkness. Every muscle in her body clenched with terror. He slanted her a sinister smile that made the hair on the back of her neck stand on end.

She braced herself for his nasty fingers to close around her, but he turned and snatched Torrie from beneath the covers. She kicked and screamed, a haunting sound that echoed off the walls and sent a spasm of nausea to Elsie's stomach. Without a word, he dragged her through the darkness into the hall, then his husky voice thundered with anger, and a slap resounded through the air.

Elsie sobbed and stood on wobbling legs. She couldn't let him hurt Torrie. She was too little, too sweet, too innocent.

Elsie had never been innocent.

She gathered her courage, then tiptoed down the hall, ducking into the corners when he paused. Surely she was wrong. Maybe they'd found a home for Torrie. Maybe someone had come to adopt her.

After all, Hattie Mae had promised them all hope when they'd been left on her doorstep.

Trying to pad softly, she continued to follow him until he reached the basement. There, her palms grew sweaty and her heart pounded. He flung open the door and threw Torrie over his shoulder. Torrie wasn't moving now, and Elsie realized he had knocked her unconsciousness.

Dear God, what was he going to do to her?

Fear piercing her, she descended the stairs in his shadow, searching the dimly lit basement, and trying to banish the image of the night she had spent in the chamber of horrors. Seconds later, he knelt in front of Torrie. "We're going to play a little game, Torrie. Do you like games?"

"She's too young," Elsie screamed. "Leave her alone, you monster!"

He pounced toward her, his eyes flashing with anger. Elsie grabbed the lantern and flung it toward him. The glass shattered, oil spilling onto the concrete floor, then it burst into flames. He bellowed with rage and sprinted toward her, but the fire shot into a mountainous blaze that caught his shirtsleeve and rippled upward. His loud horrified scream wrenched the air. Elsie jolted sideways, and ran for Torrie. She moaned, but Elsie shook her.

"Come on, Torrie, we have to get out of here!"

Torrie's eyes flickered open, then terror filled them as she saw the fire. He screamed and slapped at the flames eating his clothes and skin. Elsie grabbed Torrie's hand, and they darted away from his reach. Fire rippled along the floor, and snapped at the wooden table near the bed. The sheets and bedding exploded into flames. Smoke hurled through the air, wood popping and splintering.

He threw himself on the floor, rolling to put out the fire while Elsie pulled Torrie through the flames to escape. But fire blocked the stairwell, their only exit. "We're going to die!" Torrie cried.

Panic clawed at Elsie. Torrie was right.

There was no way out.

Chapter One

Ten years later

"Please, Deke, you have to find Mrs. Timmons's daughter, Elsie."

Deke Falcon grimaced at his older brother, Rex, and Rex's new wife Hailey. Their lives had been in an upheaval for twenty years, ever since his father had been convicted of murdering Hailey's parents. Rex had fought tooth and nail this last year to free their father, and finally, uncovered the truth about the brutal slaying of the Lyle family.

Now Hailey wanted his help. How could he deny his brother's wife after all the pain she had endured? After the way she'd blamed herself for their father's lost years when she'd suffered herself. And Rex loved her senseless so now she was family, too.

Mrs. Timmons's hand trembled as she reached for his. Anger had been his friend for the past few years, but the subtle gentleness in her touch made him want to let go of the emotion. Trouble was, he didn't know how.

"This is the last picture I have of her," Mrs. Timmons said softly. "She was only four years old when she went missing."

He studied the faded, worn-out picture, knew Mrs. Timmons had looked at it constantly the same way he had the photo of his father that he'd carried in his wallet for two decades.

Elsie Timmons, at four, was a cute kid with a gap-toothed smile, a freckled pale face and long dark curly hair pulled back in a ponytail. Her big brown eyes were almost haunting.

Where was the little girl? Had her father kidnapped her, or had something more sinister happened? Was she lost forever?

"I thought my husband took her to hurt me," she said, "but when they found that grave in the woods, I w-was certain she was dead."

"Those bones were too old to be Elsie's," Rex said.

"Which means she might still be alive and out there." Hailey's face brightened with hope. Hailey and Elsie had been childhood friends, and she had bonded with Elsie's mother.

Tears shimmered in Mrs. Timmons's worried eyes. "I...don't know if she'll want to see me," she said. "Or what her father told her about me, but I can't leave this world without trying to find her one more time."

"Hush that talk." Hailey squeezed the older woman's hands. "You're going to live forever, and Elsie is coming back to us. I just know it."

Anxiety wormed inside Deke's chest. What if he failed? What if he found Elsie and she wanted nothing to do with her mother? Or what if something awful had happened to her and he had to bring back bad news?

Could Deanna Timmons survive it?

Loyalty to her won out. She was the only person in town who'd stood beside Deke's mother when his father had been arrested. And he knew the pain of having someone ripped from his arms. His hope had dwindled with every year his father had been imprisoned just as Mrs. Timmons's hope had.

"All right. Do you have any information that might help?"

Mrs. Timmons smiled although her lower lip trembled. "I have the files the private investigator kept when he searched for her twenty years ago. At one time, he traced my ex south. I believe it was Alabama or maybe Tennessee."

She handed him a folder. "Thank you so much, Mr. Falcon. I can't tell you what it would mean to see my daughter again."

Deke swallowed hard. She didn't have to tell him. He'd felt the same way when his father had been reunited with the family.

Although nothing could replace the years they'd lost....

His chest heaved with tension as he finally looked up at Mrs. Timmons. As a falconer, he had a strong calling to the wild, to the animalistic nature within him. At times, he also experienced dark emotions, and his senses seemed heightened.

Those instincts told him that if he found Elsie Timmons, she would be nothing like the child in the picture. Something bad *had* happened when she'd left Falcon Ridge. She was entrenched in evil and darkness.

He'd have to figure out the trouble when he found her. And then he'd decide what to do with the truth.

Sweat beaded his lip as the need to flee into the woods gripped him. Thankfully, he managed to control his tremors as he shook her hand. "I'll do everything I can to find her, Mrs. Timmons."

His chest clenched at her trusting look, and he turned and disappeared outside. Seconds later, he ran through the woods, filling his nostrils with the scents of nature. Lifting his head toward the heavens, he searched the sky for the birds of prey that had come to be his friends.

Other than his brothers, they were the only ones he trusted.

The only ones that could assuage the bitterness inside him.

DEATH WHISPERED her name.

Hattie Mae Hodges clutched the bedcovers with gnarled fingers as she peered through the blackness, searching for help. In her heart, she knew it was too late. She had made a deal with the devil years ago and had no one to blame but herself.

Still, she could not succumb to the terror. And she had no right to beg for mercy.

The sense of evil whirled around her, filling the hollow eaves and shadows of the house, reverberating through each icy corner. Trees rattled and shook snow against the thin glass panes, shrouding any remaining light from the deep haunting woods that surrounded them.

The sound of a footstep broke the eerie quiet. A heavy boot. A shuffle of his gimp leg. The smell of death.

"Go away and leave me in peace," she murmured, too frail and weak now to escape her bed or his unwelcome visit.

"I warned you, Hattie Mae. You must take your promises and the truth with you to your grave."

A second later, his hands closed around her neck.

Darkness engulfed her as she choked for air, the blinding pain of his grip making her body jerk involuntarily. His sinister laugh reverberated through the room, muffled only slightly by the thick feather pillow he shoved over her face.

Images of the lost girls floated across her mind, as vivid as they were the day the children had come to her. Ann. Jessie. Marge. Carrie. Wanda. Felicity. Torrie. Elsie.

God…little Elsie Timmons.

Hattie Mae had promised them help. Redemption. Hope.

But she had let them all down.

Their terrified screams and cries of horror haunted her at night. The innocent babies stolen from their families, crying for their mothers long into the twilight. The girls' hollow, empty eyes filled with anguish as their own young were viciously stripped away, their bodies left with gaping holes where life had once grown, replaced with a pain so deep that it clawed at their insides, all the way to the cores of their very being.

All because of her husband.

No, it had been her fault.

She gasped for air, the acrid burn of her stomach rising to her throat. In her mind, the image of his charred body taunted her. God help her. She should have tried to help him.

But she hadn't. He had deserved to die, just as she did.

Her chest felt heavy. Her limbs weighted. Her head was spinning. Tiny dots of lights twirled, then faded.

Hattie Mae went limp, too close to death to struggle any longer, ready to welcome the peace if any existed.

Please, God, forgive me. I will find a way to expose the sinful secrets of Wildcat Manor, she silently vowed. *And to atone for my sins, if you let me.*

A black cauldron of despair swallowed her. She had no power in death. Her soul was lost completely.

Unless she found a way to return from the grave to haunt him.

Two weeks later

ELSIE TIMMONS STARED at the letter from Hattie Mae Hodges in shock. She hadn't heard from the woman in ten years, had not spoken to her or heard Howard Hodges's name during that time, either. But their faces and the ghosts of Wildcat Manor had followed her everywhere she'd been.

And she'd lived all over the South since. Running from town to town. From name to name. Hiding out. Trying to find her way. Trying to escape the darkness and evil that tainted her own soul.

She blinked back tears of pain and fear as memories washed over her in a blinding rush. She had to compartmentalize them as she'd always done. It was the only way she'd survived.

Then she began to read.

Dear Elsie,

I hope this letter finds you well. Unfortunately, if you've received it, it means that I'm no longer alive. I carry my sins with me, my dear, but I want you to know how much I regret letting you girls down. I know I offered you hope yet stood idly by and allowed you to be robbed of that and so much more.

God may never forgive me, Elsie, but that's my cross to bear. I don't deserve your forgiveness, but I heard that you were a social worker now. You will do the good I should have done. For that reason, I am leaving Wildcat Manor to you in hopes that you'll turn it into the kind of place it should have been.

May God be with you, child, and protect you always.

Hattie Mae Hodges

Elsie's hand trembled at the mere thought of returning to Wildcat Manor. Vivid images of Howard Hodges's body erupting into flames cut into her thoughts, the nightmares that destroyed her sleep shifting in front of her eyes. Outside, the wind howled through the mountains, the brisk temperature swirling through the thin rattling window panes, the ominous clouds threatening a snowstorm or at the least, heavy rains.

Her hand fell to her stomach as other memories flooded her. The shrill screams of the girls. The scent of chemicals and dust and…bodily fluids. The beady eyes of their tormentor flickering in the darkness as he approached in the heat of the night. The hollow feeling that consumed her afterward, the devastating pain of knowing that she had lost everything.

That she was not worthy of love.

No, she could not return to Wildcat Manor. Not now. Not ever.

Not even to try and make things right.

DEKE HAD SPENT TWO WEEKS tracking down Elsie Timmons. First to a hovel in Nashville. Then to Alabama. Then to Georgia. And now back to Tennessee to a small town set so deep into the mountains that a person might get lost forever.

But he and his brothers had expert resources. Their private investigative business had been housed in Arizona for the past few years, but with

Rex's return to Falcon Ridge, they had established a second office at Falcon Ridge.

Elsie was on the run. Never stayed in one place for very long. Which meant she was either scared or hiding something.

Determined to find the answers, he parked in front of Bodine's B & B, then made his way up the sloped, graveled drive. A view of the mountains offered a peaceful retreat for guests, the valleys and gorges behind almost as magnificent as the ones in Colorado. A handmade wreath adorned the front door, composed of dried flowers and ribbons, and a three-foot-tall metal sculpture of a covered wagon graced the porch, flanked by two rocking chairs and an empty whiskey barrel.

Maybe the case would be a piece of cake. He'd introduce himself, inform Elsie that her mother had sent him looking for her and she'd jump at the chance to go home. The hair on the back of his neck bristled, though, mocking his theory.

The cold winter wind beat at his leather bomber jacket as he turned the doorknob, the scent of pine and cinnamon apples enveloping him as he strode toward the desk.

"Deke Falcon, Miss Bodine." He tipped his head in greeting. "I'm here to see Elsie Timmons."

The owner peered at him over wire-rimmed glasses. "Don't have anyone by that name."

Damn. What name had she used here? "Can you try Elsie Thyme?" She'd used that one in school. "I'm a friend of her mother's," he said, when she continued to scrutinize him. "She sent me for Elsie."

"Oh, dear, Elsie didn't mention her folks."

He nodded, not surprised, then noted her name tag said Beverly, so decided to sway her with a lie. "Beverly, Elsie's mother's not well right now. I... thought she should know."

"Oh, of course. I hope it's nothing too serious."

Just heartsick from missing her child. "She should recover, but she's asking for her. You understand."

Beverly clucked her tongue in compassion, then visibly relaxed. "I sure do, honey. Elsie's in room five, upstairs."

Deke nodded, then climbed the steps, and knocked. Finally a woman opened the door.

For a moment, the breath was trapped in his lungs as he stared at her. While Elsie had been cute as a child, with eyes so big they had dominated her face, now she was a stunning woman. Her long dark hair lay in curls around a heart-shaped face, falling down her back, the natural highlights complemented by her gold sweater and her flowing skirt. Her skin glowed as if it had been kissed by the sun, and her lips were a natural rosy color that drew his eyes to her mouth. Such a sensuous mouth. Her lips would be soft. Supple. Tender.

She tensed as if he had offended her with his look, her long dark lashes fluttering. "Excuse me, who are you?"

He cleared his throat. Fear darkened the brown depths of her huge eyes, but shades of gold and oranges like the burnished copper of the sunset after a hot day mingled with the brown.

"I'm Deke Falcon, a private investigator," he said in a gruff voice. "You're Elsie Timmons, right?"

Her eyes widened even farther. "I'm sorry, you have the wrong room. My name is Elsie Thyme."

He stared at her dead-on, willing her to confess the lie. Instead, she shoved the door closed in his face. He stood for several seconds, then knocked again, but she refused to answer. Damn it, he shouldn't have told her he was a P.I.

Frustrated but unwilling to give up, he descended the stairs, grateful Beverly Bodine wasn't at the desk, then decided to wait outside. A short time later, he was slumped low in the seat of his Range Rover as she rushed outside with a suitcase in her hand.

She was going to leave town just as he'd anticipated. He would follow her.

And he'd find out exactly why she was on the run.

PANIC SEIZED ELSIE as she tore down the drive from Bodine's. Deke Falcon was a P.I. Who did he work for? And why had he come looking for her?

Could he possibly know about the fire ten years ago? Or some of the things she'd done after she'd left Wildcat Manor?

Had her past finally caught up with her?

Dear God, no. She had done bad things, but she was trying to make amends. She wanted to help others now. Protect the troubled kids just as someone should have protected her.

The lush mountaintops surrounded her, the small side roads and valleys offering the possibility of a place to hide. She whipped her car onto a country road that led across the mountain, then cast a desperate glance over her shoulder to see if the man had followed her.

Deke Falcon? What did he want and who was he working for? It had been ten years since she'd set Howard Hodges on fire…since she'd left him to die. Why look for her now?

Hattie Mae's death. Maybe the police had discovered something about his murder now that Hattie Mae was gone. But surely Hattie Mae wouldn't have willed her the manor if she intended to call the police on her.

Maybe her guilt had gotten to her and she wanted to make her own amends before death.

The terrifying night she'd escaped with Torrie roared back, the horrid images replacing the majestic mountain view. She and Torrie had run for what had seemed like hours. Then she'd finally found a church and dropped off Torrie, hoping someone would save the girl and give her a better life. She'd been too afraid to stay herself, had figured the police would be on her tail.

Over the years, she'd wondered what had happened to Torrie. One reason she'd decided to go into social work.

A truck roared up, zooming close to her rear, and she sped up slightly, although the curve in the road veered deep to the right, and she crossed the center line. An oncoming car blasted its horn and Elsie overcompensated. Her tires screeched, wheels locking. She skidded on the icy pavement and said a silent prayer that her car wouldn't nosedive over the barrier. The sludgy ice spewed from her tires, the gears grinding. But at the last moment, she regained control and eased it back between the lines.

Her heart racing, she glanced behind to see if the Falcon man trailed her, but once again didn't spot him, so she breathed a sigh of relief. Maybe she'd lost him.

Only he didn't look the type of man to give up. He was hard looking, tough, brusque, angry, a man who lived in the wilderness. His thick dark hair was overly long, and as untamed as a wild animal's. Dark beard stubble roughened his bronzed skin, and his mouth was set tight, as if it had never seen a smile. And his hands…they were large, dark, callused…weapons he could use to force a woman to do whatever he wanted.

A shudder coursed up her spine.

If he hadn't looked so intimidating, she would have called him handsome, but Elsie had learned long ago that men couldn't be trusted. They took what they wanted, trampled on you, then sauntered away without a backward glance.

No, it was best she had run. But where should she go now?

Hattie Mae's offer flirted with her subconscious. She'd been looking for a place to open a teen center when she'd come to Tennessee. But Wildcat Manor?

According to legends, Wildcat, Tennessee, had been dubbed the town of the damned for generations. Elsie had learned the hard way the reason for its name. The stories of ghosts and spirits that haunted the village. Of the wildcats who preyed on innocent girls, and the devil that lived in the woods. Some even gossiped that werecats roamed the area, hunting for prey.

The memory of the poor kids that she'd left behind rose to haunt her. The paper reported that all the children had survived. The orphanage had been disbanded after the fire, but she'd never been able to find out where the girls had gone.

If evil lived in the town, the people needed her to help expunge it. Maybe in doing so, she could absolve herself of the guilt that weighed on her conscience for leaving the other girls, for deserting Torrie, for her own sins....

A plan took shape in her mind. She would refurbish the place and offer hope to the young and troubled.

If she accomplished that miracle, maybe she could sleep peacefully without ghosts filling her dreams and the sounds of crying children echoing in her head, constantly torturing her. The clouds grew ominous, the wind whipping tree branches and dead leaves across the deserted mountain road as she headed toward Wildcat. Images of the monsters and overgrown wildcats popped in and out of her mind as if they were congregating in the woods to drive her away when she returned.

She clutched the steering wheel in a white-knuckled grip and perspiration dotted her face as she approached the town. Sleet slashed the windows, fogging the windshield and making the road slick with black ice. Whispers of danger floated through the air, and the daunting eyes of the devil as he waited for her return pierced the darkness.

Her nerves pinged as she parked at the deserted building. The stone structure looked even more macabre with weeds and vines climbing the sides. Burned and charred stone still covered the bottom floor wall, and the wildcat turrets flanking the massive front door practically growled into the wind. Icicles clung to the windows, hanging in jagged pointed tips that looked like swords.

Elsie's throat closed. She had run from here once and had survived. If she stepped back inside, would she survive a second time?

Chapter Two

Deke had managed to stay behind Elsie without her noticing for the two-hour drive, but her frantic escape worried him. She obviously was terrified of him, or somebody. And she was in trouble....

Just what kind? Trouble with the law? With a man? Either one would complicate his job.

Then again, maybe she'd confide in him once she learned his real reason for coming. But what if she didn't want to see her mother? What had her father told her about Deanna?

Night had fallen as she'd turned into a mile-long driveway that climbed a curvy dirt road. Snow swirled in a blinding haze, fogging his windows and creating crystals of ice that clung to the glass. Not wanting Elsie to see him, he parked in the alcove of a cluster of pines, then walked the rest of the way up the drive. Wind clawed at his face and hands, the sound of a loud growl in the woods nearby alerting him that the forest could be dangerous to some. The birds of prey who were his friends. And others....

As he drew nearer the mansion, his skin crawled. That was no ordinary house. There had been tall metal gates at the entrance, although they'd been open, and an eight-foot electric fence surrounded the property as if it had once been a prison. The gray stone structure resembled a mausoleum with turrets and a spiked chimney. There were five of them actually. A smaller stone garage was attached, a gardener's shed beside it connected by a path of overgrown weeds fighting through the snow and ice.

The sign, Wildcat Manor, indicated it had been an orphanage at one time. It had obviously been deserted for years. The boxwoods and shrubs were misshapen, weeds draped the porch and sides and a fire had burned the bottom floor caking the stone with black soot, worsened by decay and age.

What the hell was Elsie Timmons doing here?

The realization that this might have once been her home hit him in the gut. Geez, the place looked more like a funeral home than a loving place for children. Had her father kidnapped her, then left her here for some reason? Because he hadn't wanted her, or had something happened to him?

Deanna's anguished face flashed in his mind. If

her husband had been alive and left Elsie here because he didn't want her, Deanna Simmons had pined away for her daughter while the girl must have felt so alone…. And if he'd died, why hadn't someone contacted Deanna? Why hadn't Elsie tried to reach her mother over the years?

Elsie walked up the steps, her slim figure tiny next to the massive oaks flanking the drive. He watched, mesmerized by her beauty. But her face was as pale as the white snow dotting the ground. And when she reached for the door, her entire body trembled and tears flowed down her cheeks.

As hard and tough as he'd always thought himself to be, his heart throbbed with emotion.

Emotions had no place in his job.

He would not allow himself to care for a woman, especially Elsie Timmons who had run from him at first glance. She had a mother waiting for her, and he had no part in her life. He would return to Arizona when he finished here. Alone.

Back to his birds of prey and the wilderness where he belonged.

Determined to complete the job, he stepped forward anyway. He had to get to the truth, pry into her secrets and convince her to return to Falcon Ridge. Then Deanna Timmons could find peace.

And he would be done with them and could go home.

ELSIE SHOULDN'T have come. She should have driven to a hotel for the night.

But she had to face her demons or she might never be whole again. Hadn't the professors pounded that into their heads in psychology class?

Still, there were so many ghosts here, so much anguish….

The wind cut through her bones as she closed her eyes, willing her courage to surface.

You witnessed Hodges burn to death yourself. You even saw Hattie Mae standing over his grave, her head bent in sorrow. Or maybe it had been shame or relief.

Elsie had never understood how Hattie Mae had succumbed to her husband's sick wishes and let the girls suffer his cruelties.

Hattie Mae is gone, too. The house is empty, and no one can hurt you.

Elsie braced herself for the squeak of the stone door, but she shivered as she stepped inside the dark entry. The scent of dust and mildew filled her nostrils, along with fear and death. Even ten years later, the pungent odor of Hodges's flesh being charred rose with the dust motes.

Her footsteps sounded hollow on the marble floor, her erratic breathing rattling in the ominous quiet as she forced herself forward in search of a light. The electricity had probably been turned off. With the frigid temperatures, she'd freeze tonight.

No, there were the fireplaces and the lanterns.

Hattie Mae had always kept a dozen kerosene lanterns filled and ready for use when the power failed, and wood had been stacked in every room with a fireplace. As if on autopilot, she moved through the icy, cavernous living area to the kitchen. There she felt along the wall until she reached the pantry where she discovered several lanterns filled and ready for use. Matches were also stacked beside them as if Hattie Mae had been waiting on someone's return.

Elsie barely stifled the urge to turn and run. But she had been running all her life.

No more.

She would face this place and slay her demons. In honor of all the girls whose hopes and dreams had died here, she'd turn it into a safe haven for troubled teens who could find hope for a better life.

A flick of the match and the lantern lit up. Determined to overcome her anxiety, she forced herself to examine the kitchen, then the rooms on the main floor. Only leftover discarded antiques that had once shone with polish and glory remained, still sitting in the same places she remembered. The fabrics were faded, the wood dusty, the walls a dreary pea green, the paintings water damaged. She would change all that, paint the rooms bright colors, get rid of the grim furnishings and replace them with more functional contemporary pieces, sturdy ones that would turn the dark, sinister interior into a welcoming home.

Exhausted from her drive, and the tension from her encounter with Deke Falcon, she checked the door locks, pausing in the hall as she noticed the padlock to the basement. The acrid smell…

She would not go down there. Not now. Maybe never.

The memories were too painful, the images too real, the anguish and shame too raw.

Her secrets had to remain hidden.

Shaking off her paranoia, she climbed the steps, grateful for the flickering light of the lantern as she studied the print carpet, the shadows from the corners, the long hallway that led to the dormlike rooms the girls had occupied.

The room where Hattie Mae and her husband slept had been on the main floor, off-limits.

The dorm wings had separated the girls by ages. She had slept in the east wing while the kids under ten had slept in the west. She didn't think Hodges had ever ventured into the younger girls' rooms, but couldn't be sure.

Uncertain if she could sleep, she stopped at the private bedroom on the second floor. It had been reserved for the caretaker, who had seen after the girls and made certain they were tucked in at night, their doors locked securely. Elsie stepped inside, the scent of lavender and old lace greeting her. A hand-crocheted blanket covered the iron bed with cross-stitched pillow cases in blue and white. The dust that had been so evident in the house seemed minimal in here, the room clean and tidy. A white rocking chair sat beneath the window, and a full-length mirror occupied the opposite corner, complementing the antiques.

Outside, sleet slashed the roof. She built a small fire to ward off the chill, then looked out the window. Thick woods surrounded the place, trees bending and swaying with the force of the wind. The Smoky Mountains rose toward the sky like a fortress that offered a hiding place from the rest of the town.

The way Hodges had wanted it.

Back then, it had frightened her to be so far away from everyone else. Now, she sought comfort in the solitude. Keeping herself at a distance from others had saved her life in the past.

A shadow moved outside, and she tensed, studying the darkness. Was someone out in the woods watching her, or had it only been her imagination? The roar of an animal rent the air. What if the werecats were real?

No, she did not believe in the supernatural. The monsters she saw were human.

A noise inside startled her. Birds flapping in the attic? Or maybe raccoons or another trapped animal?

Seconds later, the sound of a baby crying trilled through the hollow walls. Elsie covered her ears. The sound would never cease. She heard it every night as she tried to fall asleep.

She'd run from this place to escape it, but she had never been able to. And she never would.

Because the baby had been hers. And it was lost forever.

DEKE STUDIED the orphanage, surprised that Elsie had gone inside and hadn't returned to her car. Age and weather had grayed the exterior while cobwebs and years of fallen leaves and tree branches overflowed the gutters. Weeds had overtaken the yard, the grass brittle from the winter, the windows dark and coated in layers of dirt and grime. It was as dark as Hades inside.

He couldn't imagine Elsie spending the night in the spooky place, but the fact that she had gone inside proved she wasn't as skittish as he'd first thought. Or maybe she assumed this was one place no one would ever look for her.

He considered approaching her again, but decided to wait until morning. Let her think she'd escaped him. Let her get some rest. Meanwhile, he'd do a little research on Wildcat Manor.

Then he'd catch her off guard, early in the morning before she had a chance to leave again.

Still, he watched the house until after midnight, when it grew quiet and the small light flickered off. Hunching his shoulders against the cold, he walked down the graveled drive back to his Range Rover, climbed in and followed the dirt road to the main highway. A battered sign pointed left, guiding him to the small town of Wildcat. He'd heard the South and Smoky Mountains were filled with spooky old legends. Would he find ghost stories in Wildcat?

Blinking to see through the fog, he circled the square until he found a small ten-room motel called Mountain Man's Lodge. He grimaced at the dilapidated concrete building. There was probably a cozy bed-and-breakfast the tourists used, but he didn't need frills, only answers. This truck-stop dive backed up to the woods, which beckoned him to visit for his nightly ritual.

Inside, an old-timer with gray hair, overalls and a hearing aid lifted his frail hand in a wave. "I'm Homer. You ain't from around these parts, are you?"

He shook his head no. "I need a room for tonight."

"Just passin' through?"

"I'm not sure how long I'll be here."

Homer handed him a key to room nine, then

looked him up and down. "You never been to Wildcat before?"

"No. What can you tell me about the town?"

The old man huffed. "Don't many people that come through here ever come back." A chortle rumbled from his thin chest. "Fact is, some of 'em never leave, either."

"You mean they like it so much, they settle?" Deke asked.

"Not hardly." Homer gestured out the window to a small white chapel at the foot of the hills. "See that cemetery? That's where they end up. Damned just like the town."

Deke frowned, wondering if the man's comment had been a warning. Then again, Homer didn't look dangerous.

"The devil lives in those woods along with wildcats as big as tigers, some of 'em half-human," Homer continued. "Call 'em werecats. They feed off animals and humans."

Homer must be senile. "Then why are you still here?"

He pointed out the window toward the hills. "Buried my wife, Bessie, a few years back. Cancer got her. We were together forty-five years. Can't bear to leave her here alone."

Deke frowned. He had no idea love and devotion like that existed anymore. Of course, his parents had weathered their own terrible storm and wound up back together. "I passed a place called Wildcat Manor coming in," he said, putting his personal thoughts aside. "It used to be an orphanage?"

The man's thin skin stretched over his bony jaws as he frowned. "Yep, but they closed it down ten years ago. Bunch of troublemakers lived there, didn't associate with the townsfolk. Strange things went on in that manor. Stories about young girl runaways. The old man was crazy."

"What happened to him?"

"Died in the fire that destroyed the basement of the building. The orphanage was disbanded then. Reckon his wife, Hattie Mae, was too scared of the hellions they put with her." He wheezed a breath. "Rumors said one of the girls set the fire."

"What happened to Hattie Mae?"

"She died a few weeks ago."

"Did you know a woman…a girl actually, named Elsie Timmons? Was she one of the orphans?"

"Didn't know any of them by name," the man said. "Hodges never let the girls come into town, thought they'd stir up too much trouble with the decent young boys." He scratched his chin. "To tell the truth, most of 'em were troubled, had been sent there by the law or cause their families didn't want 'em. The town sure as hell didn't."

Anger sparked in Deke's chest. How could the

people in town have been so cruel to homeless kids? To Elsie?

And someone *had* wanted her—her mother. Only Elsie might never have known.

The tragedy of his own lost years with his dad rushed back, yet somehow Elsie's situation seemed worse. He had to convince Elsie that her mother wanted to see her. He would go tomorrow.

His mind set, he accepted the key from Homer, retrieved his bag and let himself into the small motel room. The furnishings were minimal, the furniture old, the drapes and spread faded. He didn't care.

He stepped outside, ignoring the brutal weather as he slipped into the dark wooded mountains. He'd see Elsie tomorrow. Find out why she was running. Tell her about Deanna.

Tonight he had to regroup. He couldn't let Elsie's sad story get to him. He was a loner. A falconer who needed no one. Who could not afford emotion. He had his own rituals. His own secrets.

Nature called his name, begging him to return to the wild where he belonged. He had to answer.

SOMEONE WAS IN Wildcat Manor.

A young woman. He had watched her enter from the safety of his woods, and wondered if she was a stranger or if she might be one of the lost girls who'd finally come home. He'd figured that some day one of them might return. Looking for Hattie Mae.

Wanting answers.

Or revenge.

The abject fury in the thought sent a burning pain through his hunched shoulders. Wind whipped through the thin layer of his jacket and clawed at his aching bones.

He had vowed to Hattie Mae that he would keep the secrets of Wildcat Manor safe. That no one would ever find out about her weakness. And if this girl had come to snoop around or expose them, he wouldn't hesitate to stop her.

No matter the consequences.

Forcing himself to remain in the shadows of Hattie Mae's life had been torture, yet she had always known he was there. That if she needed him, all she had to do was whisper his name. That she was never far from his mind or his watchful eye.

This girl would learn that she wasn't welcome.

Now. It was almost dawn. Time of the awakening.

A smile slid onto his wind-parched face as his boots sank into the thick snow. Slipping through the back gate came easily—he had done it a thousand times. Even sought refuge from the cold behind those monumental stone walls. Tonight would be no different.

Clenching his jaw, he eased his way through the

basement, his eyes automatically adjusting to the darkness, the sounds and smells of the dank space and the rituals that had been performed there rushing back as if time had stood still. He could still see the young girls pleading for their lives. The children who had been turned by the devil. The sinners who had to pay.

Hattie Mae watching in horror.

It was her fault, though. Hers and the bad children.

Pungent odors filled his nostrils, and warmth slowly seeped into his freezing body. He ascended the steps, remembering the night Howard Hodges had died. It had been a night just like this. Bitter cold. Complete darkness.

The wooden rungs squeaked, the sound of a mouse skittering beneath the furnace causing him to grin as he opened the door leading to the main hallway. Like a cavern, the house was completely void of light, but the scent of freshly lit kerosene wafted from above, and he realized the woman had found the lanterns. How had she known where they would be?

She had been here before. It was the logical explanation.

So which one of the pretty children had returned to the lair?

He slowly padded up the steps, his hand shaking as he focused on his plan, his mind spinning with the names of the orphans who'd stayed at Wildcat Manor, with the sounds of their cries and pleas, with the vulgar truth of their pasts. With their tempting eyes....

The dim glow of the lantern drew him closer to the bedroom, and he paused to listen, then heard sheets rustling and a whimpering sound as if a child had returned, not a woman. Pulling his cloak around his face and over his arms, he moved to the doorway and watched.

Her long dark hair was curly and lay across the pillow. So erotic. It had been a long damn time since he'd held a woman. She thrashed from side to side as if in the throes of a nightmare.

A chuckle threatened to erupt but he tamped it down. Didn't she know that by coming here her nightmare had just begun? Like a voyeur, he hid in the shadows and watched her struggle for sleep, but no peace came. She muttered nonsensical panicked sounds, clutching the sheets with clenched fingers, perspiration trickling down her honey-lit skin.

Then he recognized her.

Elsie Timmons.

Rage and fear warred with the need to hold her. His hand trembled. His pulse quickened. Sweat beaded on his neck and rolled down his back.

Suddenly, she jerked awake, eyes wide in the darkness, wild with confusion and fear. A shrill scream pierced the air when she saw him, and his instincts drove him forward. He pounced on the bed, covered her mouth with his hand, then shoved a pillow over her face. He desperately wanted to kill her. And he had to protect the secrets at Wildcat Manor.

She squirmed and clawed at his hands, but he chuckled.

No, killing her now would be too easy. She deserved to suffer.

Yes, he'd draw it out, torment her, make her feel the pain for a while.

Then he'd put an end to her....

Chapter Three

"Leave Wildcat Manor or die."

Panic pumped through Elsie. The man's acrid breath brushed her ear, and he loosened his grip on the pillow slightly. "Let the dead rest in peace," he murmured. "Or you'll be one of them."

Icy fingers of fear tore up her spine, and she tried to wrench herself away. The years rolled back as if it had only been seconds since she'd run from Wildcat Manor.

The devil was in the house and he'd come to get her. Unspeakable horrors awaited.

He slid one hand down to her throat. His fingers dug into her skin, and Elsie summoned her fighter spirit. She'd found it the night she'd murdered Howard Hodges. And on the streets she'd practically become an animal.

She had to act now. A second longer, and he would cut off her windpipe completely.

Gathering her strength, she thrust her elbow up

sharply, catching him in the ribs. He yelped and loosened his hold at the unexpected blow. Taking advantage of the opportunity, she spun around and stared at him, trying to see his face, but a long black cloak shrouded her view. He lurched forward, but she jabbed his eyes with her fingers, then rammed her fist into his belly. He bellowed in pain, grabbed her hair and yanked her head so hard pain rippled through her scalp. Then he flung her across the room. Like a beast, he shot toward her with a roar.

She scrambled away, reached for the fire poker and swung it sideways at his legs. The metal end hit him in the groin, and he doubled over. She jumped to her feet and ran from the room, down the steps, nearly tripping in her haste.

Outside, the wind howled and rain pounded the ground. She grabbed her purse and ran toward her car in her pajamas. Barefoot, the ice stung her feet, sharp pains knifing through her toes. Running as fast as she could, she jumped inside her car and locked the door. Her hands shook as she tried to insert the key. It jammed. Good grief, she had it upside down! She had to hurry!

The roar from the porch bled through the haze of fear, and she glanced up to see the creature running toward her. She cried out and tried the key again, hands trembling. But this time she got it in and the engine sparked to life.

He raced after her, his cloak billowing around him, but she gunned the engine and flew down the mountain.

DEKE JERKED AWAKE with a start. Something was wrong. He sensed it.

Rising quickly, he jerked on a pair of jeans, boots and a denim shirt, then grabbed his coat and headed into the wooded mountains. Were the birds of prey in danger? Were there werecats preying on others or was the old man senile?

No, Elsie was in trouble.

He'd felt an instant connection with her just as he did with some animals, as if his sixth sense told him they were now bonded.

He considered driving straight to the orphanage, but decided he'd scare her to death if he appeared at her door this early. He could go in on foot, though, and watch the house. Wait for the sun to break through the clouds. Then pay her a visit.

Snow and ice crunched beneath his feet as he hiked deep into the forest and climbed toward Wildcat Manor. Inhaling the fresh raw scent of pine and winter, he paused to check the area for any injured animals, but saw nothing. Yet he sensed the evil. The predators. That there might be wildcats hiding behind the trees, sneaking through the forest. Or hybrids—human animals…

The uncanny feeling that Elsie was in danger here in Wildcat hit him again, this time so strong he began to jog.

Nearby, animals scrounged for food in the bed of ice and dead leaves. The piercing eyes of a wild animal, maybe a bobcat or mountain lion, caused him to pause, and he searched the trees for predators. Was the old man at the motel right? Were there strange creatures in these woods? Was the devil really hiding behind the shadows of the caves and snow-laden trees?

He came to a ridge that jutted out overlooking the valley, giving him a clear view of Wildcat Manor, which was only a quarter mile above him. He stepped onto the precipice, sensing the hollow emptiness below and the churning tide of tension in the area. Secrets. Evil. The town of the damned.

He had to know what had happened here.

He scanned the mountain property housing Wildcat Manor and glimpsed a swish of black feathers flying along the top of the house. Vultures. They squawked, falling into predator mode, circling and spiraling downward toward the chimney as if they had just found fresh fodder.

His stomach clenched. Elsie. Years of honed instincts roared with the certainty that she was in trouble.

Adrenaline kicking in, he sprinted up the hill. Veering between the massive trees and brush was second nature, expecting the worst a nightmare that dogged him daily. What if something had happened to Elsie last night? Or this morning?

What if he'd misjudged her and she'd run again or someone had hurt her? What would he tell Deanna?

He increased his pace, climbing higher, higher, ignoring the biting cold and brisk wind. He was one with the birds.

The metallic taste of death sent a flood of bile to his throat. He had to hurry.

PANIC ROLLED THROUGH Elsie in waves. Where could she go now? What should she do?

The tremors intensified as she remembered the dark-cloaked attacker, but she quickly banished them. She was alive. She had fought him off.

And she was going to survive. No one was going to scare her away.

But she needed protection.

She'd buy a gun today, install dead bolts on the doors and get the power connected so she wouldn't have to live in the darkness.

For now, she needed coffee to warm her and help her stop trembling. But she couldn't go inside the town café wearing her pajamas. There was an all-night diner on the edge of town with a drive-through window. She headed toward it, slowing her pace as the rain intensified. Another car met her at the foot of the mountain, and she blinked, tensing as it approached. But the sedan flew by her, and veered onto another street that led to the river.

Her breathing finally steadied as she approached the diner. The temptation to go inside where she would be safe taunted her. Yet no one in this town had helped her ten years ago. Why would she think they might now? And if she told the police…

They might look into her story. Maybe her past. And she would go to jail for murder. Now that Hattie Mae had died, there was no one to verify that she was telling the truth. Admitting to killing Howard Hodges would be foolish.

Shivering at the thought of that horrible night, she rolled down the window at the drive-through, wishing she had a coat to hide her predicament.

A balding middle-aged man with a missing tooth narrowed his eyes at her momentarily, then grinned. "What can I do for you?"

She shuddered, then realized he probably assumed she was picking up coffee for her and an overnight lover. Let him think what he wanted. She'd long ago lost a good-girl's reputation. Survival was all that mattered.

"A large coffee," she said.

"Breakfast with that, ma'am?"

Her stomach was churning too badly to eat. But she'd need something later. In her haste to escape Deke Falcon, she hadn't stopped to shop.

"Yes, a…a biscuit and sausage.

"Coming right up."

She dug in her purse and handed him a twenty. With a toothless grin, he dropped the change into her hand, then shoved the food toward her.

She placed the paper bag on the seat beside her, taking a small sip of her coffee as she pulled away from the window. Still shaken, she parked in the corner and tried to calm herself before she headed back to Wildcat Manor.

She'd come too far to turn back now. Her destiny was here, she knew it.

Her breathing rattled in the quiet as she started back up the mountain a few minutes later. Dawn broke the sky, but dark storm clouds obliterated the light. When she pulled up to the manor, her heart clenched. Could she really face her demons?

Yes, she had to or she'd be hiding out the rest of her life. And she didn't want to hide out. She wanted a life.

She took a deep breath, circled her hand around the mace in her purse, grabbed the food and coffee and climbed out, scanning the woods and property as she neared the porch. The forest seemed ominous, shadows clinging to the thick rows of trees, but she saw no one. Her heart racing, she slowly walked up the steps, listening for sounds that her attacker had returned.

Suddenly a man stepped from the shadows.

Deke Falcon. Tall. Imposing. His dark expression was hooded. But his eyes flared with questions.

He squared those broad shoulders, making him look even more intimidating. So he had followed her to Wildcat. Did he know about her past?

A shudder splintered through her.

Was he the man who'd attacked her?

"ELSIE?"

"What are you doing here?" she said, although her voice came out a mere whisper, fading in the wind.

"I have to talk to you." He narrowed his eyes, wondering why in the hell she was outside, had been driving, in her pajamas. His gaze fell to her feet, and he grimaced. She had to be freezing. Her toes were red, the sharp sting of cold flushing her face, and she was trembling.

"Were you in my house earlier?"

He shook his head. "No, why do you ask?"

She shrugged, her teeth chattering, the coffee cup in her hand wavering.

"Come inside and get warmed up," he said in a gruff voice. "I swear, I'm not here to hurt you."

Her chin jerked up, a wariness there that cut him to the bone. Women had been scared of him before. His family history. His size, his brusque manner, his frown—he knew he looked cold, that women found him imposing. It had never bothered him before.

But Elsie looked like a small kitten, and he felt like an ogre knowing that he'd frightened her. What had happened to make her so distrustful?

"You followed me," she said in an accusatory voice, making no attempt to go inside or come near him. "I want to know why."

"I'll explain when we get inside." He removed his faded leather jacket, then lifted it in offering to her. She shook her head, and anger hit him.

"For God's sake, Elsie, I'm not going to hurt you. I came here to help you." His mouth clenched when she backed away. But he managed to catch her, then slid the coat around her trembling shoulders. "Come on. I refuse to stand out here and watch you freeze. Your feet are going to be frostbitten."

Her mouth parted in a small strangled sound, but he ignored it and coaxed her up the steps and inside. The interior was dark, and she set the bag and coffee down, then grabbed a lantern. He took it from her and lit it.

"Is the power off?"

"I'll have it connected today."

"I'll build a fire then."

She hesitated, but he ignored her as he glanced around to find the den or parlor, whatever they called it in this monstrosity. Old dusty furniture, macabre paintings and cobwebs made the place feel dreary. And a collection of stuffed wildlife including a hawk, a mountain lion and a raccoon occupied the corner near the fireplace. Anger surged through him at the sight. He wondered how she'd stayed here the night before. Or ever.

A stack of wood by a fireplace in the room to the right drew his eyes, and he strode toward it. Within seconds, he'd built a fire. The warmth from the blaze lit the room, knocking off the worst of the bitter chill.

Elsie moved near the heat, keeping a safe distance, but shrugged off his coat. She quickly grabbed a blanket off the sofa and wrapped it around her, still hugging the coffee to her, but curling within it as if the blanket and fire offered her protection.

"Why were you out in your pajamas?" he asked.

"I…someone broke in and attacked me this morning," she said in a faint whisper. "W-was it you?"

He swallowed hard. He'd never been good with women, but the fact that she thought he might have attacked her made his gut churn. Still, he lowered his voice, containing his emotions. "No, Elsie. I stayed at the inn down the road. Mountain Man's Lodge. You can call and ask Homer if you want." He cleared his throat, more alert. "Did he hurt you?"

"No…I'm okay." She rubbed at her neck and his gaze fell to her pale skin. Bruises marked the edge of her collarbone and neck.

He gritted his jaw. "Did you call the police?"

"No."

Panic tightened her face, and he frowned. He reached for the cell phone clipped to his belt. "Do you want me to call them?"

She stared down into her coffee. "No…please don't."

"Why not?"

She self-consciously tried to hide the bruise with her hand. "I just don't trust them," she whispered.

He gave her a clipped nod, although her fear of the police raised his suspicions. Why wouldn't she report the attack? Was she in trouble with the cops?

"Would you tell me if you had broken in?" she asked quietly.

"I'm not a liar," he said in a gruff voice. "And I'm going to search the house to make sure he isn't still here."

Her eyes widened when he bent over and retrieved his gun from the strap beneath his jeans. "What is that for?"

"Protection. I don't intend to meet an intruder unarmed." Ignoring the fear on her face, he stalked through the rooms, his senses on alert. First the drab kitchen, then the dining area, then the master suite. There was no evidence that Elsie had stayed in the room, making him curious. But the dark furnishings, lack of natural light and old-fashioned furnace reminded him of Falcon Ridge when he was growing up. Now, Rex had renovated the place and updated it, it had a homey feeling, not as daunting as the stone walls that their mother had hated.

Slowly he padded up the stairs, pausing every few steps to listen. He'd half expected Elsie to follow, but she must have decided she was safer in the den away from him, close to the front door so she could run if she needed to. The realization stung, but he ignored it. Why did he care what Elsie Timmons thought of him?

He veered to the left and found a wing composed of two large bedrooms that appeared to be dorm rooms for the orphans. Several small cots lined each pea green wall, the faded gold spreads and dusty furniture a sign that the place had been deserted for some time. The walls were scarred, a threadbare ratty yellow curtain hung askew, and a battered wooden toy box sat in one corner. An image of lonely children locked in the glum rooms brought a flash of sympathy. Had the toy chest ever held toys? Had the children celebrated Christmases and birthdays and gotten presents?

Had Elsie been one of those kids? He had to find out why she had come here....

He found a similar wing to the right, then a smaller private bedroom that actually felt more normal. The furniture was oak, not new, but not weathered like the children's rooms. He scanned the corners before entering, then realized Elsie had slept in this smaller room. The unmade bed indicated she had left in a hurry.

Had the man attacked her here?

He stepped forward, and examined the rumpled bedclothes, but saw nothing that might identify her attacker. A suitcase was open in the corner, and a small travel bag sat on the floor in the bathroom, but there was no intruder. Anxious to get back to her, he noticed a door to an attic, but it was locked on the outside, so the intruder couldn't have entered through it. He also spotted a similar lock on the basement door on the main floor.

She glanced up at him when he entered, still wary, but at least she had stopped shivering. And she hadn't run, either.

"I didn't see anyone. Do you know how he got in?"

A curtain of her long curly hair fell across one cheek. "No."

"Were the basement and attic doors locked last night?"

She shivered visibly. "Yes. They stay locked."

He walked back to the fire and started to kneel in front of her, but she drew back her shoulders and he paused, keeping his distance. He had to win her trust if he was going to convince her to return to Falcon Ridge with him.

"Did you see what the man looked like?" he asked.

Her eyelashes fluttered, and she sipped the coffee. "No, but he had the devil's eyes," she said in a low voice.

He frowned. "And you thought it was me?" Anger hardened his voice this time as the memory of his father being falsely accused of murder raced back.

She shrugged. "You are following me. I…still don't know the reason."

He heaved a breath. If she believed the tales about the devil living in the woods and thought he'd attacked her, maybe she wasn't quite stable. How could he take her back to Falcon Ridge like this? Deanna Timmons would be devastated.

"Either tell me or get out," she said, her voice stronger.

He nodded, considered a lie, but that wouldn't be fair and would only prolong the process. He needed to know if she wanted to go home to see her mother. Then he could decide what to do.

"Your mother hired me to find you."

Elsie gasped, a strained silence stretching between them. She'd almost gotten her trembling under control, but the cruelty of his statement triggered another onslaught. Her hand shook so hard she sloshed coffee over her fingers and had to set the cup down. His eyes pierced her. But he said nothing, simply waited.

Pain so raw and deep she felt as if she'd been sliced open tore through her. How many times had she told herself it didn't matter that her mother had sent her away? That no one wanted her?

Elsie finally found her voice, although she hated the tears that laced it. "You're lying," she choked out. "Why are you doing this to me?"

He arched a black eyebrow. "I'm not lying, Elsie. It's true. She sent me to find you."

The anger she'd relied on for years resurfaced to give her strength. "My mother is dead," she snapped. "Now, get out of here."

Chapter Four

Elsie stood, willing Deke Falcon to leave her in peace. Not to open doors to the past that held pain so intense she'd once thought she'd die from it.

But instead of moving, his black eyes pierced through her as if he could see all the way inside her soul. "Who told you that your mother was dead?" he asked in a low voice.

She clutched the blanket tighter around her shoulders. "My father. Now, I asked you to leave, Mr. Falcon."

"It's Deke, Elsie." He tried to reach for her but she backed away. "And your mother is not dead. She's very much alive and she wants to see you. She still lives in your old house in Tin City."

A bitter laugh escaped her. "Now I know you're lying. My mother sent me away years ago, back when my friend Hailey died."

A long tense second followed. "Hailey is alive, too." His voice dropped a decibel, almost apologetic as if he thought she'd already known. "Everyone thought she was dead, but she came back to Tin City a few months ago."

"What are you talking about?" Elsie whispered. The memory of the night Hailey had disappeared hung like a dark cloud, still vivid in her mind. In spite of the fact that her mother had warned her to stay away from the Lyles, she had crawled into the attic to visit Hailey earlier that day. But she'd left when Hailey's daddy had come home. Hailey's father had been cruel and abusive, and the two girls had both been terrified of him. Elsie had felt guilty that she'd abandoned her friend.

"Hailey and her family were killed that night," she said. "By the caretaker who lived next door. His name was…" She hesitated, then suddenly the name shot into her head. "Falcon…. Mr. Falcon…."

Harsh lines slashed his jaw as he scowled with anger. "Yes, Randolph Falcon, he was my father."

Dear God, Deke Falcon's father was the hatchet killer.

Fear bolted through her. Why had he come to her now?

She took a step backward, but her foot hit the hearth, and she nearly tripped. He grabbed her arms, but she wrenched away. "Please don't hurt me. Just leave," she pleaded.

"I told you, I'm not here to hurt you, just like my

father didn't hurt anyone," he said between clenched teeth. "Your mother sent me to search for you. She wants to see you. The night Hailey's parents were killed, your father took you away. Your mother has been looking for you ever since."

Elsie staggered, unable to accept his declaration as true.

"It's a long story, Elsie, and I'm not leaving here until you hear me out."

She swallowed hard, trying to remember Deke from childhood. There had been three Falcon boys, all older than her, all mean as snakes. Their father raised falcons, and the school kids claimed the boys were strange, that they communed with wild animals.

Deke removed an envelope from his shirt pocket and pushed it toward her. "Look at these. They're pictures of Hailey's wedding. She married my brother, Rex. Your mother attended the ceremony."

"Now I know you're fabricating this story. If Hailey returned, she'd never marry the son of her family's killer."

Deke closed his eyes as if she had stabbed a knife in his chest. When he opened them again, pain had settled in the dark brown depths. "My father didn't kill Hailey's family. That's what I'm trying to tell you. Rex, Brack and I run a P.I. firm. Last year, we reopened my father's case and when

Hailey returned, they discovered that she'd repressed memories of the murder."

"It turns out that Hailey's father had a twin brother. He came to help Hailey, her mother and brother escape the abuse, but Hailey's father showed up and killed the mother and son. Hailey ran into the woods. Everyone thought she had died, but she climbed into a small boat and a trucker found her later. She had lost her memory and wound up in foster care. When Hailey came back to Tin City, her father, who'd been hiding all these years, tried to kill her. My brother saved her."

Hailey's sweet face flashed into Elsie's mind, and tears filled her eyes. "Oh, my God. You're serious, aren't you?"

"Yes, Elsie. My father was cleared. Hailey and Rex married." His solemn eyes spoke the truth.

Elsie's head was spinning. Hailey was alive. Mr. Falcon hadn't killed Hailey's father.

If that were true, maybe Deke was telling her the truth about her mother.

"Look at the pictures, Elsie. The proof is there. Hailey and your mother are both alive, and they want very much to see you."

Elsie stumbled backward and collapsed on the hearth, letting the heat from the fire warm her back as she opened the envelope. Inside, several photos fell into her lap. In the first one, she was small, about four or five years old, with a missing front tooth and a big smile. A memory crashed back, the day her mother had taken the photo. They'd gone shopping and had ice-cream sodas at the soda shop in town. Then her mother had bought her a charm bracelet. What had happened to it?

She jerked her head toward Deke. "Where did you get this?"

"Your mother gave it to me. She kept it all these years." He hesitated, his voice gruff. "That's the way she remembers you, Elsie, as the little girl she loved."

A low sob caught in Elsie's throat. "I…can't believe this is happening, that all this time…"

Deke gestured toward the other photos. Two tall muscular men who resembled Deke flanked a gorgeous woman. "That's Hailey now," Deke said. "And my brothers, Rex and Brack, on Rex's wedding day. Hailey planned to remodel her old house into an antique shop, but it burned down. They're living at Falcon Ridge now, while they build a new house on her old property."

Elsie's mind raced to assimilate the information. Her best friend from years ago was really alive. She had survived her awful childhood. And now she looked so happy. Tears trickled down her cheeks, and she swiped them away, hating to reveal her emotions in front of Deke Falcon. He seemed so angry.

She thumbed through two more pictures of the wedding, until her gaze fell on a group shot. An older woman with graying hair and the warmest smile Elsie had ever seen stood in the center.

"That's your mother, Deanna," Deke said in a gruff voice.

Elsie pressed her hand to her mouth to stifle a cry. She'd recognized her immediately. "She's... so beautiful." Elsie's heart stammered. Although she was smiling, the woman's eyes held an emptiness, as well, as if she had experienced deep sadness in her life. The kind of loss that Elsie had felt in her own heart since her father had taken her away.

Could it possibly be true? Had her mother really wanted her?

Memories bombarded her. Memories she had stored away in the most distant corners of her mind because they had been so painful. She and her mother weaving pot holders out of yarn. The two of them baking a cake for her birthday. Her mother singing lullabies to her and tucking her into bed.

Her mother had loved her. Elsie had felt it back then.

A woman like that wouldn't just turn her back on her child. Her gaze met Deke's, and she saw the truth in his eyes. But her smile faded as bitter reality surfaced. Her father had lied to her all these years. He'd convinced her that she was responsible for the plague of death on Hailey's family. That her mother hated her. And later when she'd grown up and had questioned him about her mother, he'd claimed her mother was dead.

Then Elsie had been even more lost. Even more confused and angry. And she'd gotten in trouble.

So much trouble that she'd blamed herself when her father had abandoned her to the horrors of Wildcat Manor.

DEKE HAD ALWAYS BEEN a sucker for a damsel in distress. And Elsie Timmons fit that picture perfectly. Instead of happy or excited, she appeared to be tormented by his news.

Of course, he understood her mixed reaction. He had been thrilled that his father was released, but the bitterness he felt from all the time he'd lost with him, for all the pain his family had endured, especially his mother, had lingered.

Elsie had obviously struggled. If her claims were true, her father had lied to her all her life. Where was he now?

She studied the pictures over and over again, then glanced back into the fire, dazed. Her eyes looked haunted, grief and sadness so embedded in the depths, that his gut clenched. She reminded him of the injured animals he and his brothers found in the wild. A butterfly maybe, or a wounded kitten.

"Your mother wants me to bring you back to see her," he finally said.

Her gaze flew to his, questions and worry flashing.

"I'll be glad to escort you."

"No…I can't go."

His anger rose, defenses born from a lifetime of being looked at as a killer's son surfacing. Was she still afraid of him?

"You can call her yourself." Furious at himself for wanting to soothe her pain when she looked at him as a villain, he reached inside his wallet, removed his business card, then scribbled her mother's name and number on it. "This is my P.I. firm, if you want to check it out, and there's your mother's number."

Her chin quivered as she accepted the card. "She really wanted me all these years?"

The anguish in her voice overrode his anger, and he sat down beside her and gently touched her hand. A frisson of sexual awareness bolted through him, the sight of her eyes filled with tears nearly ripping him inside out. "Yes, Elsie. Call her. She'll be thrilled to hear from you."

She clamped her teeth over her trembling lip. "I…can't right now. I need time, time to think, to take all this in."

He stroked her hand with his fingers, aching to pull her into his arms. A possessive, foreign feeling he didn't understand filled him. "Where is your father, Elsie?"

Fear and something else—shame? anger?—settled across her face. "I don't know. I haven't heard from him in years."

"What happened after he took you from your mother?"

She glanced down at her hands, at his fingers as they moved slowly over hers, but she didn't pull away. "We moved around a lot. Every town he took me to, we used another name."

"Your mother hired another P.I. back then," he said. "But your father managed to stay hidden."

"He didn't…couldn't keep a job," she said. "He blamed her for their failed marriage, for me."

"What do you mean?"

She couldn't explain the painful things he'd said to her. "I…I don't think he wanted a child."

"But he stole you from her," Deke said in a low voice.

"To hurt her," she said, raw pain tingeing her voice.

He muttered a curse, and she averted her gaze, rocking herself back and forth. "When was the last time you saw him?" Deke asked.

The shaking that had finally stopped racking her slender frame assaulted her again, and he ground his teeth to keep from putting his arms around her. He had to move slowly with Elsie, be gentle, approach her as he would a wounded hawk.

"When I was fourteen."

He frowned. "What happened?"

She shook her heard, hunching her shoulders. "I...don't want to talk about it."

He gestured around the monstrous room. "He left you here at this orphanage, didn't he?"

A slight nod of her head served as her reply. Then she stood and turned toward the fire, seemingly lost in the flames.

"I will take you back to your home," he said. "When you see your mother, everything will be all right. Trust me, you'll see."

Elsie shook her head, tears spiking her long black lashes. "It's too late," she said in a haunted whisper. "I can't go back now, Deke. Not ever."

Raw anguish knifed through Elsie. In mere seconds, she'd memorized her mother's features. Her smile. Her sad eyes. The changes in her face. The slight graying of her hair.

And with that, the memory of her voice had returned. The sound of her soft singing. Her spontaneous laughter. The smell of the gardenia lotion she used on her hands. The look of joy on her face when Elsie had drawn a picture for her or when she'd done something to please her mother.

"I'm so proud of you," her mother would say. "You're my little angel."

But in the fire, Elsie saw Howard Hodges, his skin burning, his eyes screaming in pain, the flames eating his hair.

If her mother knew what Elsie had done, how she'd survived, the fact that she had murdered a man, she couldn't smile or be proud of her. And she would never call her an angel.

Shame would fill her eyes. Disappointment. Maybe fury.

She would send Elsie away for sure this time. Elsie wouldn't blame her.

She wasn't the innocent, sweet little girl she had been when she'd lived at home or when she'd played hopscotch and baby dolls with Hailey. But heaven help her, she wanted to go home. Wanted to feel her mother's arms around her.

She angled her face and saw Deke studying her. She had been afraid of him when she'd first met him. Yet in the last few minutes, he had shown her a tenderness she'd never known existed. A tenderness between a man and a woman.

He had made her want to fall into his arms and let him hold her. Yet his raw masculinity frightened her at the same time. How did she know if she could trust him?

He was only here doing a job. And it was

sympathy in his eyes, not real emotion or caring. Or even attraction.

No, if she confided about her past, he would never want to be seen with her. He might even turn her over to the police.

He placed his hand on her arm, turned her to face him. "Elsie, talk to me. Tell me what's going through your head. I swear, I'll help you."

She pulled away, immediately missing the warmth of his touch. But she couldn't share her horrid secrets with anyone.

"I need some time to think."

"To think about what?" His voice sounded gruff, slightly agitated. "Deanna has called me almost every day the last two weeks to see if I've found you. She'll want to know what you look like, when I'm bringing you back." His dark brows furrowed. "I hate to lie to her. She's a sweet lady, and she's suffered for a long time."

Guilt weighed on Elsie's shoulders. She almost wavered. Deke Falcon had no idea how much she wanted to see her mother. But she couldn't return until she made something of herself. Until she faced her past and rectified her sins by building this center for kids. If she didn't, she would always look at herself as an evil person.

And as a murderer.

Chapter Five

Frustration filled Deke. He'd expected Elsie to hear him out, then let him drive her back to see her mother and a happy reunion to ensue. Then his job would be done.

It was obvious that Elsie wanted to see her mother. She was plainly devastated to learn that her father had lied to her. So why would she choose to stay in this mausoleum where her father had left her? What kind of hold did the town have on her?

He had to dig deeper. Find out what had caused her to be so skittish. Why she had come back here. What she was hiding.

"Elsie, tell me why you really don't want to go back to Falcon Ridge." He started to reach for her again to assure her that everything would be all right. But her shoulders tensed and she drew away, his touch unwelcome.

"I…just can't," she whispered in a faint voice.

"Why not? Do you have obligations here in town? A job or a man in your life?"

"God, no," she whispered.

"Then what?"

"My mother doesn't know me now," she rasped. "I'm...not the same little girl she once had."

No. She was a stunning woman. Delicate and vulnerable with eyes that mesmerized him, and a soft pouty mouth that he desperately wanted to kiss. No, he wouldn't do that.

But someone had attacked her, and he had to protect her for Deanna's sake.

And for his own? He couldn't deny that he'd instantly felt drawn to her. Maybe because he understood the pain of desertion.

Except that his father hadn't deserted him of his own free will.

Still, at times, Deke had blamed his dad for not being around. For staying away so long. For not fighting harder to beat the conviction and get it overturned.

The silent realization shocked him. He shoved his hand through his hair, trying to make sense of his reaction. He'd never given voice to those irrational feelings before. And they were irrational—his father had been innocent. He'd tried his damnedest to free himself, but the truth hadn't mattered.

Although when he'd been sentenced, his father

had refused to see the boys. Deke had thought he didn't love them anymore.

As an adult, he understood that his father had been trying to protect them. He hadn't wanted his sons to see the meanness inside the prison. He'd thought the family would have a better chance of happiness without the turmoil of constant prison visits tainting their impressionable lives.

But Deke *hadn't* understood at the time. He'd been devastated and hurt, had felt as if his father had abandoned them completely. And he'd hated hearing his mother cry at night, had felt so helpless….

But his parents love for each other had survived, and now the family had been reunited. Deanna and Elsie deserved the same.

"Elsie, your mother loves you," he said gruffly. "Nothing that's happened in the last twenty years can change that."

Her gaze met his, and his gut clenched at the pure fear and pain darkening her eyes. She didn't believe him.

"I…I have to do something here first," she said in a raw whisper.

He stroked her arm, relieved when she didn't pull away. "Then I'll help you."

She shook her head. "You can't," she said softly. "No one can." Gathering the blanket tighter around her shoulders, she gestured toward the door. "Now please go, Mr. Falcon."

"Deke."

She sighed, a tired sound that yanked at his heart more. "Deke. Please, I need to be alone."

"What do you want me to tell your mother?" he asked.

The question appeared to shake her barely controlled equilibrium. "Tell her that you can't find her little girl, that she's still lost."

"I won't do that," he said in a rigid tone. "Her little girl is right here, and she needs her mother as much as her mother needs her."

Fire flashed in her eyes. "What are you, Deke, some kind of therapist?"

He barked a laugh at her display of anger. "No, just someone who knows what it's like to lose a parent as a child. All those years my father was falsely imprisoned…" His voice cracked slightly. "I…needed him. Even as a man, I still do. I'm not ashamed to admit that."

Emotions glittered in her eyes like raindrops, ready to fall in the prelude of a violent storm.

"Please," she said quietly. "Let me be alone now."

He stared at her for a long moment, but finally gave a clipped nod. An injured bird needed time to rest. Time to heal. To learn to trust. So did Elsie.

"My cell phone number is on the card I gave you.

Call me if you need anything." He hesitated. "Especially if someone tries to hurt you again."

She traced her finger over the edge of the card. "I'm sure I'll be fine. Goodbye, Deke."

Elsie had no idea who she was dealing with. Deke Falcon couldn't be run off so easily. "I'm not leaving town, Elsie," he said in a low voice. "Not until you're ready to go with me."

He didn't wait for a reply. Instead, he strode to the door, a smile creasing his mouth at the surprise on her face. Elsie Timmons might be stubborn, but she needed protection and help. And he was a man of his word.

Wherever she went, he would be right behind her.

As soon as Deke Falcon left, Elsie locked the door behind him. The well of emotion she'd tried to bottle overflowed, tears running down her cheeks like a river.

She let herself cry it out. All the loneliness she'd lived with for so long had been needless. Being spirited from town to town, changing names, never making friends, being shut up with her father while he drank himself into a stupor. All for nothing.

How many nights had she lain in bed, unable to sleep, wondering why her mother didn't want her? Why her father didn't love her.

Then he had deserted her, too.

Rage unlike anything she'd ever known exploded inside her. How could he have been so cruel?

She doubled over, pain rocking through her. Her father had hurt her mother, destroyed all their lives because he'd been a selfish bastard. And all this time she had blamed her mother when her mother was suffering. She might have even thought that Elsie's father had hurt her.

Her poor mother. She traced her fingers over her features in the photo. Age had made its voice known by the tiny wrinkles and lines around her mouth and eyes, and her hair had streaks of gray, but Elsie loved her as if they had never been apart.

Memories of the orphanage returned like macabre snapshots in a tattered memory book. All those horrible lonely nights. The evil Mr. Hodges. The other children. The babies....

If she had lived with her mother all these years, she would have never known that world existed. She would have been loved. Would have attended a normal school, enjoyed girlfriends. Maybe a boyfriend....

And she wouldn't have turned to the streets for survival. For any crumb of affection a boy or man had to offer. She might have even been happy. Fallen in love. Gotten married and had a family of her own.

If it hadn't been for the Williamsons, the last family who'd taken her in, there was no telling what would have happened. But the woman had encouraged her to finish school, to get an education. And, thankfully, she had listened.

An image of Deke Falcon's face replaced the bitter memories, but she quickly banished it. What man would want her when they learned the truth about the woman she'd become?

No. Her chance for love and a family ended long ago.

But she could make amends to the other girls and right the wrongs being done to children by opening the teen center.

Her heart hammering in her chest, she hurried to the bedroom and removed the silk embroidered handkerchief her mother had made for her when she was little. She had cross-stitched Elsie's name on it in yellow and added a small butterfly in the corner. Elsie had almost thrown it away when she'd thought her mother had died, but it was the only thing she had left of her. She sniffed the handkerchief, remembering the sweet scent of her mother's hand soap.

Determination and strength filled Elsie. She would not let anyone run her off until she turned this place into the safe haven it should have been, until she had something to be proud of.

Then she would return to Falcon Ridge, see her mother and pray that she'd forgive her.

FROM THE RANGE ROVER, Deke's gaze tracked the broken bits of stone, the decay and rot around the scarred basement, the dead leaves and twigs swirling along the overgrown yard of the manor. The frosted windowpanes held layers of grime, ice and fog that hid the dirty secrets within the walls.

His stomach knotted at the thought of Elsie inside the monstrosity alone. What if the person who'd attacked her returned? And who had the intruder been? A homeless person seeking shelter? Someone from her past who'd followed Elsie here? Or someone who didn't want Elsie in Wildcat Manor?

He had to persuade Elsie to confide in him. But how?

Maybe if he discovered the real reason she'd returned to the manor, he would understand Elsie's compulsion to stay here. More detective work was in order.

He glanced at his watch, the dark sky growing more ominous, the shadow of the sun trying to burst through the clouds, but unable to, as if light never shone on Wildcat Manor.

Duty called. He had to report back to Deanna with an update on his progress. She'd be on pins and needles waiting.

Sweat beaded on his forehead, the truth too cruel

to tell her. *I found her, Deanna, but she refuses to come and see you.*

No, he could *not* relay that harsh reality. And he didn't understand Elsie's motivations enough to lie. Another concern teased the edges of his mind, spiking worry. At this point, taking Elsie back to Colorado might endanger Deanna.

His head throbbing, he phoned Rex instead.

His brother answered on the second ring. "What's up, Deke?"

That was Rex, always to the point. No chitchat or beating around the bush with small talk. "You might tell me how the family is before you give me the third degree."

"Everyone here is fine. Anxiously awaiting your return." Rex chuckled. "Now, do you feel better?"

Deke laughed. Rex had changed since he'd married. Solving their father's case and meeting Hailey had freed his brother of his rage. Before, Deke couldn't have imagined Rex cracking a joke. "Yeah. I want to make sure you guys are missing me."

"We're falling apart without you."

"Yeah, right." Deke chuckled again, then heard Hailey's voice as if she'd come up next to his brother. Damn, they were mushy.

"So, spill it," Rex said, more serious. "What's going on?"

Deke exhaled. "I found Elsie."

"Jesus." Relief tinged Rex's voice. "Hailey and Deanna are going to be thrilled."

"You can't tell Deanna yet, Rex."

A tense second lapsed, punctuated by a heavy sigh from his brother. "Why not? She is alive, isn't she?"

"Yeah, she's alive." Deke silently cursed. But her soul had been shattered. "It's a long story, but the bottom line is that Elsie isn't ready to come home."

"I don't understand."

Deke rubbed a kink in his neck. "When I finally confronted her, she ran. Then I followed her to a small town in the Smokies called Wildcat. Let me tell you, brother, this town is creepy. The locals claim werecats live in the woods."

His brother's lack of comment told Deke the rumor might be true. After all, they'd grown up in the mountains, and in the woods, all kinds of wild animal life took shape.

"What's she doing there?" Rex asked.

"Staying at an old abandoned orphanage."

"An orphanage? What's that all about?"

Deke hesitated. "Elsie lived there when she was younger."

"You mean Deanna has been looking for her and she was at an orphanage?"

Disgust mushroomed inside Deke. "That's right.

Her old man stole her from her mother, then moved them around from town to town. He kept changing their names and IDs so no one could trace them."

"Where is he now?"

"She didn't say, and I don't think she knows. He dumped her here when she was fourteen."

"So he may still be alive?"

"Maybe. She hasn't heard from him since he deserted her."

Rex released an expletive. "I'll get Brack to hunt for him. If or *when* we find the SOB, Deanna can file kidnapping charges."

Abuse charges, as well, Deke guessed, but he refrained from comment.

Rex cleared his throat. "So what did she say when you told her about Deanna?"

"The truth upset her. Elsie's old man told her that her mother didn't want her. And later, he told her Deanna was dead."

"Damn." Rex hissed.

Deke squinted toward the woods. He thought he'd seen a shadow. Could it be Elsie's attacker or one of the wildcats?

Seconds later, a deer pranced through the opening, and he released a pent-up breath. "Elsie claims she needs time to think," he finished.

"To think about what?" Rex asked. "I can't believe she doesn't want to hop on the first plane out here."

"I think she's in trouble, Rex. She's frightened and secretive. Definitely running from something."

"From the law?" Rex paused.

"I don't know. Maybe an old boyfriend." Deke twisted his mouth in thought. "Someone attacked her last night in the manor."

"Geez. Did she report it to the police?"

"No, she refused to. Another reason I'm suspicious."

"Right, be careful," Rex warned. "And don't let anything happen to her, Deke. It would kill Deanna."

"I know. I'll play bodyguard until I can figure out what the hell's going on here."

"Good. Just watch her. Keep her safe. Earn her trust."

"Winning her trust is not going to be easy, Rex. She's terrified of something." Or someone.

"It wasn't easy with Hailey, either. But it was damn worth it."

"That was different," Deke argued. "You and Hailey…you had a personal connection from the beginning."

Rex chuckled. "Yeah, that was different."

His sarcastic tone set Deke's nerves on edge. "I don't intend to get involved with Elsie," he said in a stony voice. "I'm only doing this for Deanna."

"What does she look like?" Rex asked.

Deke frowned, remembering that long curly

hair. Those mesmerizing eyes. Those sweet kiss-able lips.

But he'd messed up by getting involved with a client once before and gotten screwed, and he wouldn't do it again.

"Like her picture but she's older."

"All grown up, she must be a beauty."

"I'm hanging up now," Deke said, ignoring his brother's ragging. "What are you going to tell Deanna?"

The sound of Rex rapping his knuckles on the desk echoed over the line while Rex contemplated his answer. "I'll tell her that we talked and that you have a good lead."

"Thanks." Deke snapped the phone closed. What had he said that had given Rex the impression that he was attracted to Elsie?

Elsie was just a case to him. A beautiful, myste-rious one, but he would walk away when he took her home. Just because his brother claimed to have met his mate for life, didn't mean *he* would.

Through the open car window, the sounds of the woods intensified from behind the manor, and his heart pumped faster, heat and blood spiking. The faint echo of an animal's cry for help chilled the already frigid air, and the sound of another animal giving chase in the woods followed. Heavy paws pounded the earth, then the swish of brush and bramble as it raced through the dense foliage. The wild was calling his name again.

No woman would ever understand his need. Ever fulfill that part of him.

He was a loner. A man who liked to be on his own. A man who belonged with the birds and animals.

Not tied to a woman.

But Elsie resurrected other needs he couldn't meet in the wild or alone. The need to hold her, to share heat, flesh against flesh. To feel her lush body, to pound himself inside of her and make her scream his name in the throes of passion.

To mate with her as the wild animals did, fast, furious, with no barriers.

But the price of loving someone was too painful.

And some needs had to be left unmet. Because some animals lived alone and belonged to no one but the forest.

Just as he did and would continue to do so long after Elsie Timmons had gone home.

BURT THOMPSON PACED the confines of his law office, tension knotting his neck as he stared out his window at the rolling hills and snowcapped mountains. "You're sure it's Elsie Timmons?"

"Yes," Dr. Mires snapped. "She stayed at Wildcat Manor last night. I told you not to send the will to her."

"I didn't," Burt argued. "Hattie Mae must have had someone else mail her a letter."

He wheezed a breath. "Then again, the Timmons girl hasn't contacted me yet, so maybe she isn't here to take ownership of the house. Maybe it's a coincidence."

"A coincidence, my ass," Mires growled. "You know good and well that's baloney. She hasn't been back in ten years."

"Maybe she just returned to pay her respects to Hattie Mae."

"Or to divulge what happened there years ago." Mires released a string of expletives. "We can't allow that."

"Don't you think I'm aware of the danger?" Burt barked.

"Then what are we going to do?"

"Give it a day or two. I'll see if she contacts me, then find out her plans."

"We have to get her to leave town as soon as possible," Mires said, his voice laced with worry.

Burt poured himself a scotch on the rocks and downed it, his hand shaking. "I understand. I'll take care of the problem."

"You'd better. And Burt?"

"Yeah?"

"It has to be final this time. Pay her off big-time or something."

Burt laughed silently. Mires had no guts. Bribery would only make her come back for more. No, they had to get rid of her. Elsie Timmons would not expose them. And if she started asking questions about Hattie Mae's death, if Elsie realized the old woman hadn't passed of natural causes, that she'd been murdered…

No, she'd never find out the truth.

He tossed the highball glass into the fireplace and watched it shatter. The fire burst higher into the hearth as if it might explode. Just as trouble would if the truth were revealed.

The truth will set you free, his mama used to say.

But the truth would not set him free. Hell, it would destroy him and the others.

Just as they would Elsie Timmons if she didn't go away.

Chapter Six

The chill of the bedroom ignited memories of the earlier attack, but Elsie refused to allow the incident to deter her from her mission in Wildcat. She spent several hours cleaning and dusting the house, then had to wash up. Doors secured, she turned on the shower, praying for hot water, but without the furnace working, an ice-cold spray splattered her hand. Shaking her head with frustration, she wrapped her bathrobe around her, grabbed her cell phone, checked information and located a fuel company that promised to deliver fuel for the outdated radiators within the hour. The call to the electric company came next.

And finally, the call to Burt Thompson, the lawyer who'd handled Hattie Mae's affairs. She needed to inform him that she was responding to Hattie Mae's wishes. Then she'd go into town and search for hired workers to help her get the place in shape.

She wanted to complete the project as soon as possible.

He answered on the third ring. "Mr. Thompson?"

"Yes, who is this?"

She considered using a fake name, but as far as she was aware, no one in town had knowledge of the orphans' names. Besides, she needed her legal name in order to claim the property.

"My name is Elsie Timmons."

A long pause followed.

"Mr. Thompson?"

"Yes. I'm surprised to hear from you."

A sliver of unease tickled her spine. "You know who I am?"

"Of course. I handled Hattie Mae's will."

"Yes, well, I've come back to Wildcat Manor because of her."

Another silence.

Elsie frowned. "Hattie Mae sent me a letter and suggested I use the manor for a teen center I'm planning to open."

"Let me warn you, the town was not enthusiastic about having an orphanage of troubled kids here years ago," Thompson said in a curt tone, "and they won't be now."

His comment stung. Elsie remembered vividly how some of the people in town had treated the girls. The orphans had been considered bad, sinful, dangerous. The adults had been afraid of them, while the teenagers had taunted and called them ugly names. The old familiar shame washed over her, but anger replaced it.

"Mr. Thompson, I'm aware of the town's history. But certainly the people have progressed past their small-mindedness."

Thompson's breath hissed out. "How dare you."

She inhaled sharply, mentally preparing for battle. "I'm not a frightened teenager now, Mr. Thompson, and I won't be intimidated." She paused for a response, but his sullen silence vibrated with anger, so she continued. "Most of the girls at the orphanage had family problems and needed love and attention, not to be judged and shunned. Perhaps if someone had taken the time to care about them and help them, they might have turned out to be valuable citizens who could have contributed to the town."

"They nearly burned the orphanage down," Thompson snarled. "And that fire killed the very man who took care of them."

Bile collected in Elsie's throat. If only he knew the truth about what Mr. Hodges had been like. "I wouldn't call what Mr. Hodges did to the girls taking care of them," she said tightly.

"Are you finished with your diatribe, Miss Timmons?"

Elsie fisted her hands. "Just one more thing. I believe if I appeal to the locals' Christian values and humanity, they'll offer their support. There have to be some caring individuals in this town, and I intend to find them."

"Well, good luck there." His tone was as cold as the brutal wind outside. "But don't say that I didn't warn you, Miss Timmons. And just so you know— a few nosy people have come searching for information about the orphanage before and well…they either disappeared or ended up dead."

Elsie shivered at the deliberate attempt to frighten her.

Her fingers went to her throat, massaging the bruised skin, the memory of the attack returning. The feel of the man's hands closing around her neck. The scent of his breath against her ear.

The whine of a baby's cry echoed from the eaves of the house, and screams of fear and helplessness followed. All memories or ghosts lingering?

Yes, danger was here. It vibrated in the air. But she would change things and build the center so the lost ones could find redemption.

And no one, not Thompson or even the devil, would stop her.

DEKE'S TREK INTO THE WOODS rejuvenated him. He'd searched the forest, using his keen senses to determine if the rumors about the mountain lions and werecats were true, but he hadn't caught sight of them. Still, an unknown scent of evil permeated the air, just as it had when he'd walked past the basement in Wildcat Manor. Whether its source was human or supernatural, he didn't know.

He stomped ice from his boots as he climbed into his SUV, and glanced at the manor one more time. He hated like hell to leave Elsie alone, but she obviously didn't intend to share her secrets with him. He'd have to investigate on his own. She had his number. If she needed him, hopefully she'd call. He couldn't very well stalk her.

If he pushed too hard, she'd run again.

Dark skies covered the mountaintops, the tremor of trees shivering a reminder of how deadly the elements could be. He shifted into gear and drove slowly across the icy road in town to the center of Wildcat. A metal sign with the name of the town and an etching of a bobcat dangled in the wind, supposedly welcoming visitors.

But he didn't expect them to welcome Elsie or his questions.

The old faded storefronts desperately needed paint and boards replaced, the roads had potholes that needed filling, and the few folks who had ventured out this morning rushed along the town square, battling the wind, their shoulders and heads hunched inside bulky winter coats. A small white church sat at one end of the square, the jail and sheriff's office ironically opposite. A general store offering both hardware and groceries occupied the center of town, surrounded by a hair salon, gun shop, antique store, fabric store, gas station and a drugstore. He noticed a café called Wildcat Crossing at one corner, and turned into the parking lot, hoping to get a hot breakfast and some answers.

The minute he entered, he felt as if he'd walked into a time warp. Two old-timers wearing overalls played checkers in the corner over a table made from a whiskey barrel. Pictures of covered wagons, railroads and the mountains dominated the pinewood walls, and an ancient cash register held station at the checkout counter. Two white-haired women sipped iced tea from mason jars. The menu sported everything from homemade biscuits with sausage, red-eye gravy and country ham, to chicken and dumplings and chitlins. He frowned. He never actually believed people ate chitlins.

The scent of hot coffee drove him forward to the counter. Two men dressed in suits glanced at him, but when he met their gaze, they quickly turned away. A few others stared openly.

A pudgy white-haired woman approached him, snagging the pencil from her hair. "What would you like, mister?"

"Coffee, and that country lunch special."

"Ham or sausage?"

"Ham."

She poured him a cup of coffee, then shouted the order at a skinny man wearing a stained white apron and hat.

"Where're you from, mister?"

He read her name tag. Norma Jo. "Colorado."

Her eyes shot up, and he realized that forks had stilled and others had tuned in to listen. Strangers in town must be an anomaly. How many of the folks here knew Elsie? And of the ones who did, who knew she had returned?

"What are you doing here in Wildcat?" Norma Jo asked.

He sipped the coffee. "Traveling through."

"Through to where?"

He ground his heels into the floor. He was supposed to be asking questions, not answering them. "I haven't decided yet. But I've heard things about this town that intrigue me."

She cocked her head sideways. "How long do you plan to stay?"

Until he could convince Elsie to leave with him. He shrugged. "I don't know. Haven't decided." The cook handed her his plate, and she slid it in front of him.

"Actually, I've done some real estate developing,

and I found this abandoned building up the mountain. Wildcat Manor. I'm thinking of buying it."

Curious, wary looks flew back and forth across the room. "What the hell you want with that old place?" one of the men from the checker game asked.

Deke shrugged. "I'm not sure. Maybe I'll turn it into a hotel."

"Fat chance you'd have getting anyone to spend a night there," a curly haired woman said. "It's haunted."

"Really? What else can you tell me about it?"

"It used to be an orphanage," the man playing checkers offered.

Norma Jo fidgeted with her uniform. "Yes, until one of the kids set fire to it. Killed the man who ran it." She sighed, her eyes rolling skyward in memory or disgust. "Miss Hattie Mae closed it after that. She couldn't handle those bad kids alone."

Deke nodded. "Yeah, Homer told me about the fire. He also said the man's wife died recently. Who owns the place now?"

Norma Jo shrugged. Everyone else remained silent.

"Did Hattie Mae will it to someone in her family?" he asked.

"She didn't have any family," the elderly woman said. "Died all alone. So sad after she tried to help those children."

"What about the girls she took in?" Deke asked. "Some of them must have been close to her."

"They were mostly runaways," the woman on the other side of the counter said with a huff. "Sinners, thieves, liars. The state sent some of them to her. Poor Hattie Mae tried to help 'em, but some kids are just born bad." She hesitated. "To tell you the truth, I think Hattie Mae was scared of some of them."

"Why? Did one of the kids hurt her?" Deke asked as he bit into a fluffy biscuit.

"She never would admit they hurt her, but she always had bruises," another lady offered.

"And a black eye once or twice." The curly haired woman shivered. "Some of us tried to have the place shut down to protect her, but we never were successful."

Deke frowned. "Did they find homes for the children when the orphanage was disbanded?"

A hush fell over the room. A few patrons dropped their heads, pretending renewed interest in their food.

Finally, Norma Jo answered. "Mister, people who adopt want little ones, babies, not dangerous kids with criminal records, or a pregnant teen to take care of."

A short pudgy man in a police uniform lumbered up beside Deke, his thumbs tucked in his belt loops. "You sure do ask a lot of questions." He angled his head toward Norma Jo. "I think you've blabbed enough, woman."

"But Wally—"

He cut her off. "Get me some coffee and the usual."

Her face blanched, but she whipped around and began scouring the counter. Silence stretched taut across the room.

Deke shot the sheriff a cold look. "She was only making conversation, Sheriff, offering a little Southern hospitality."

"We don't like nosy strangers in our town." His voice boomed in the silence. "Especially when they ask questions."

Deke swallowed back the urge to punch the man in the face. "Why not, Sheriff? If I opened a hotel here, it might help business."

"Nobody wants that old place opened up," the sheriff snapped. "And we don't want you here, either."

"I didn't come to cause trouble," Deke said.

"To hell with that lie," the sheriff snarled. "I know who you are. You're a damn private investigator."

Deke's eyebrows shot up. So the man wasn't as ignorant as he looked. "I see you did your homework."

"Damn right I did, boy. It's my job to protect the people in this town."

Deke ground his teeth. Bitter memories of

another small-town sheriff assaulted him—seeing his father questioned by the man, falsely accused of murder, then railroaded to jail. The older kids calling his dad a murderer. The girls running from him and his brothers, saying they were dangerous, just like their daddy.

The sheriff leaned closer, so close Deke smelled his coffee-and-cigarette breath. "Now if I was you, I'd get out of town."

Deke tossed some cash on the counter for the meal, then shot Norma Jo a grateful look. "No one tells me what to do, Sheriff. When people slam doors in your face, they're usually hiding something." He jammed his face into the other man's, saw a vein throb in his forehead. "Now get this straight. I have no intention of being run out of town."

He strode toward the door, his boots clicking across the wooden floor like thunder. It was obvious the man knew more than he was telling. Deke would break him one way or another.

Cold air nipped at his skin as he stepped onto the porch, shrugged into his bomber jacket and scanned the streets. The wind hurled a tree limb to the ground, then the limb sailed and bounced across the icy street like a tumbleweed blowing through a deserted ghost town. What had happened here to make the town so damned spooky and secretive?

Several hundred feet down the street, he noticed

Elsie climb from her car. She tugged a coat around her and rubbed her hands together to keep warm. She looked small and lost, and so damn beautiful it nearly sucked the air from his lungs. He imagined her being given the same treatment he had and shuddered. There was no way he'd leave her here alone. Not after that run-in with the sheriff.

He clenched his jaw and headed toward her, remembering the attack on her the night before. If the sheriff wanted to guard town secrets, and he knew Elsie had returned, would he try to frighten her off?

ELSIE DUG her gloved fingers into her coat pocket, battling the elements as she hurried toward the gun shop. She didn't intend to spend another night in Wildcat Manor without protection.

Then she'd check the hardware store for supplies and a handyman to help her with the renovations. The fabric store should have material for new curtains and furniture covers. Her budget was limited, but her small nest egg might suffice.

And of course, she had to go the courthouse and secure the deed to the manor. Since the house had already been used as an orphanage, surely she wouldn't have problems with zoning. It was far enough away from town that the residents couldn't protest, especially when they read her proposal for the center. A big game room for teens to hang out and recreational activities. Counseling services. And maybe she could coordinate planned parenthood classes and offer private consultations in conjunction with the local hospital.

She stepped up to the sidewalk to cross the street and joined a small cluster of residents waiting for the light to turn red.

Suddenly someone shoved her from behind. She screamed, her arms flailing as she struggled to regain her balance. Her boot caught in a crack in the asphalt, and she lurched forward. Her palms hit the ice a second before her knees slammed into the concrete. Pain shot through her body.

A second later, she glanced up in horror. Tires screeched, and brakes squealed as a pickup truck raced toward her.

Chapter Seven

Dark clouds swirled in the bleak sky, threatening rain or another ice storm. But shouts and screams from the sidewalk pierced the air over the noisy rumble of thunder. What the hell was going on?

Where was Elsie? He'd lost sight of her....

"He's going to hit her!" someone yelled.

"Oh, my God, get up lady!"

Deke's pulse pounded as he catapulted into motion. Through the throng, he spotted Elsie on the ground, and raced toward her. That truck was only inches away. If it hit her now...

No, he couldn't let her die. What would he tell Deanna?

"Get out of the way!" He vaulted over the curb and fire hydrant, cut through two teens on the street gawking, then swooped down and grabbed Elsie. He dragged her to safety a second before the truck would have hit her. It finally screeched to a stop, metal and the icy sludge from the street spewing as the massive vehicle slammed into the fire hydrant. Water gushed upward, sending everyone nearby screaming and running in different directions.

He clutched Elsie to him and dragged her to the sidewalk. Her voice cracked on a sob, and her eyes were glazed with shock.

"You're okay now, Elsie," he whispered, cradling her cheek in his hand. Her gaze latched onto his for a long minute, and his heart pounded. "It's all right. I've got you."

She clung to him, and he held her tightly, hugging her so his warmth could console her.

A teenage boy jumped out and ran toward them, flushed and wide-eyed. "Are you okay, lady?"

Several people hovered nearby, watching curiously as Deke checked her over for injuries. Sheriff Bush stalked toward them, and Deke grimaced as the man shot him a suspicious look.

"What happened out here?"

A middle-aged redhead twisted her scarf around her neck. "That woman fell into the street."

"No, she jumped in front of him," a man shouted. "Must have been trying to kill herself."

"He was driving too fast!" an older woman screeched.

Sheriff Bush zeroed in on Elsie's face, one graying eyebrow arched. "Ma'am, are you all right?"

Elsie nodded, although tremors racked her slender body, and blood dotted the palms of her hands and knees where she'd hit the pavement. "I didn't fall...." she whispered.

"What?" Deke stroked her arm, and pulled her closer.

"Someone pushed me," Elsie said in a shaky voice. Deke's jaw tightened as her gaze swept the crowd. He angled his head sideways and did the same, searching for someone running away.

Sheriff Bush folded his arms across his chest. "You're saying one of our citizens intentionally pushed you?"

Elsie nodded, but anger churned in Deke's throat at his skeptical tone.

Bush patted his belt. "Don't suppose you happened to see this person?"

Elsie stiffened. "No, he shoved me from behind."

Bush spread his arms in a wide arc toward the locals. "Did anyone here see Miss Timmons get pushed?"

A chorus of nos rumbled through the group, and they hunched deeper in their coats, distancing themselves from the scene.

"It was crowded," a gray-haired man with a beard said as if in defense. "Everyone started to cross the street at the same time. She probably got nudged, lost her balance and *thought* someone pushed her."

Deke scanned the locals. Women and children. An elderly man. Two teenage girls.

The pickup truck driver bent over, still panting as sweat rolled down his pimpled face. "I swear, I tried my best not to hit her, Sheriff. She just came out of nowhere."

"You stopped in time, son. But I'll need to file a report and get this fire hydrant repaired." He punched in a number and spoke to his deputy, but the fire truck screeched up before he even made the request. Firefighters jumped off, vaulting into action.

"Let's break it up now." Bush waved a hand toward the crowd urging them to go about their business, and one of the firefighters helped clear the street.

Elsie composed herself. "How did you know who I was, Sheriff?"

"Talk spreads fast in a small town," Bush muttered.

"So you know I intend to reopen Wildcat Manor and transform it into a teen center?"

The man cut a scathing look at the two of them, and Deke realized that Elsie was still huddled close to him. She must have realized it at the same time and pulled away.

"Like I told your friend, Mr. Falcon," Bush said with a leer, "the townsfolk don't want Wildcat Manor reopened. So get your things and get out of town before there's any more trouble."

ELSIE'S THROAT THICKENED with emotions. Fear that the sheriff had just threatened her. Anger at him for not taking her seriously.

Someone *had* pushed her. She hadn't imagined it.

He put a hand on the truck driver's shoulder, and they moved to the pickup truck.

Deke led Elsie to an overhang, away from the prying eyes of strangers and the brutal wind. He checked her over once again, then slid a hand along her cheek. "Are you all right?"

"Yes, but I don't like the sheriff."

"Neither do I," Deke growled. "He's hiding something."

Elsie nodded. Although the last thing she wanted was to drag Deke into her problems. She certainly didn't want him investigating her past.

He gently lifted her hand and examined the scrapes, removed a handkerchief from his pocket and dabbed away the blood. Elsie stared at his strong jaw in silence, amazed at the tender way his big hands touched her. His fingers were large, long with blunt-tip nails, his shoulders broad and muscular. He could crush her if he wanted. And his masculinity was nearly overpowering. Yet, she had never felt such gentleness from a man.

His dark eyes rose to meet hers, and for a second, locked. A tingle of sexual awareness rippled through her, tightening her stomach into knots. She wanted him to kiss her. To stroke her lips with his tongue and draw her back to him so she could feel the solid wall of his chest, the heat in his powerful body.

"Elsie, please leave this town with me," he said in a gruff voice. "Let's go back to Tin City and see your mother. You're not safe here, and we both know it."

She tensed. She had never felt safe anywhere. Not with her father or the Hodgeses or on the streets. Her nightmares haunted her, along with the shame and memory of the awful nights in Wildcat Manor, of that last fateful night when she'd caused the death of Howard Hodges. His scream of pain and horror screeched through her head as it had a million times over the years. But Torrie's cries echoed as well, making her heart clench. She'd done the right thing, even if it had meant she was a murderer.

Sure, her mother wanted to see her, but she didn't know Elsie now. If she did return, she'd have to keep her secrets hidden, because no one could love the person she'd become....

Her entire life had been lies. Lies from her father. From the Hodgeses. Broken promises.

And the lies she'd told on the streets....

She had to break the cycle. Could not return to her mother with more lies on her tongue and conscience.

She yanked her hand from Deke's, knowing she

couldn't trust anyone. As a kid, she'd fantasized about a white knight in shining armor rescuing her, but white knights only rescued fairy-tale women, and she wasn't a princess. She had to rescue herself.

"Elsie, please. You don't need to stay here. It's not your home."

"I can't go back yet, Deke. I already told you that."

He dropped his hands to his side, and cold seeped through her, the absence of his warmth making her ache for him to hold her again. But she couldn't give in to that need.

"You keep saying that, but you never explain the reason." He raised his finger and stroked the side of her face. Tears threatened at his gentle caress, but she choked them back.

"I don't have to explain anything to you," she whispered.

She backed away, but he held her arm, then forced her chin up with his thumb so she had to look into his eyes. His breath kissed her cheek, his hot look sent heat rippling through her.

"Whatever you're running from, whatever you're afraid of, I'll protect you." His voice sounded so sultry, that she almost believed him. "And Deanna will understand, Elsie. She's your mother, she loves you."

The thought of disappointing her mother tore at her emotions. "Go back to her, Deke. Make her understand that I will come to her one day when I've put everything behind me."

Deke's jaw tightened, the wind ruffling the layers of his dark brown hair. "If you don't tell me what happened, I'll find out on my own, Elsie. I'm not leaving you here in this hellhole alone. It's too dangerous."

She stepped backward, determined to drive him away. She couldn't bear for him to know her secrets. "Stay out of my past," she said, her voice shaking. "Or I swear Deke, I'll leave town and disappear, and you'll never find me."

SHERIFF BUSH FINISHED with the young driver of the truck, then headed straight to Thompson's law office, his day going downhill fast. He greeted Thompson's secretary, Donna, with a grin, wishing like hell she'd leave her husband for him. All this sneaking around wore him out. He had enough secrets to keep without worrying about hiding out with the woman he loved. If it weren't for that damn kid of hers, she'd leave the jerk, but he had practically blackmailed her into staying.

A worried look tightened her slender face. "Wally, I heard there's a woman staying at Wildcat Manor."

Man, news traveled fast in small towns. "Yes. Elsie Timmons."

"Oh, my heavens. The Elsie Timmons who lived there, the one who gave birth to—"

"Hush, Donna. Don't worry. I'll take care of things just like I did back then."

She worried her lip with her teeth. He ached to kiss her anxiety away, but he couldn't touch her here, not in town.

Damn it. "I'm going to talk to Thompson now."

Her eyelashes fluttered as if she'd read his mind and wanted his touch, as well. "He's in a foul mood," she said.

"Aren't we all?" Not bothering to wait for her to announce his visit, he knocked on Thompson's door, then charged in.

The lawyer glanced up from a desk full of paperwork and the phone, his agitated expression almost comical. But nothing was funny about the Timmons girl's return. Her presence could rock Wildcat Manor to the core, open up old sores, expose raw secrets, destroy families and ruin lives.

Thompson motioned for him to wait with a raised finger, and Bush gave him a look that said he wouldn't tolerate waiting.

"There's nothing you can do about rezoning?" Thompson asked. A pause. "All right." He slammed down the phone with a vicious thud.

"What was that about?"

"I was trying to stop Elsie Timmons from opening Wildcat Manor as a teen center, but I haven't had any luck with zoning."

"So you know she's here?"

Thompson ran a hand through his thinning hair. "Yeah. She's trouble."

"It gets worse." Bush paced over to the window. He could probably scare off Elsie, but with that Falcon man… "She's got some damn P.I. from Colorado with her asking questions. We have to put an end to it now before they discover something."

Thompson reached for a drink. The fact that he had indulged this early in the day told Bush the lawyer was nervous.

"Maybe you should threaten her with arrest. You have evidence that she set the fire that killed Hodges, don't you?" Thompson inhaled his scotch. "Or hell, if you don't, fabricate some."

Bush swung around and rested his palms on the desk, leaning forward. "I thought of that, but if we arrest her, she's bound to spill everything."

Thompson's face blanched. "You're right. We can't let that happen. Have you talked to Mires?"

Bush shook his head. "Not yet. But I imagine he's pretty damn worried. Hell, he could go to jail for what he did."

"And I would lose my license."

"I doubt you'd get off that easy," Bush said in a

harsh tone. But his stomach churned with worry. *He* would lose more…his job, his family…everything.

Thompson snapped his fingers, his eyes perking up. "Mires doesn't have the guts for this. It's up to us."

A smile creased Sheriff Bush's face. "You're right. So get on it."

Thompson nodded. Bush didn't ask any questions. The less he knew about the details the fewer lies he'd have to tell.

DEKE HEADED to the small town library to search for answers. As much as he'd wanted to follow Elsie all day, he had heard the desperation in her voice, and knew he had to back off. Hell, he was afraid she'd run away again. And the thought of that, and her in danger, tore him inside out. Why, he didn't know.

He wasn't supposed to care about Elsie. Just bring her home.

What could make her so desperate that she would flee rather than face him and admit what was frightening her?

Had it been the physical connection between them when he'd brushed Elsie's cheek? He wanted to forget the case, drag her in his arms and hold her to him until she trusted him. Until she confided the truth. Until she let him kiss her and obliterate her pain with mindless pleasure.

He shook himself from the haunting spell she had cast over him. It wasn't personal. He was simply worried about her because of Deanna. Naturally sex had entered his mind. To a man, comfort meant sex, physical bonding. To a woman, to Elsie, comfort meant safety—which meant she wanted him to stay away.

The truth clawed at his ego. That was it. Nothing more.

He would find out everything about her, then figure out a way to help her. The sooner he ended this case, took her back home and returned to Falcon Ridge, the sooner he would get his head back on straight again. Women were trouble— trouble to be avoided.

The faded dusty library books, outdated encyclopedia collection and ancient computers raised his doubts about the educational system in Wildcat.

A thin woman wearing a Minnie Mouse shirt and bifocals approached him. "Sorry you had to wait. I was just finishing up with the children's story hour."

The reason for the shirt, he guessed. "No problem, ma'am, I just got here. I'm interested in old articles about the town. Specifically anything to do with Wildcat Manor."

She tapped her fingers on the desk, her friendly demeanor disintegrating. "Why do you want to know about that old place?"

"Just curious. I've heard some interesting rumors since I arrived in town."

She leaned closer, her eyes darting around as if she feared someone was watching them. "Wildcat Manor is haunted, has been for years, ever since old Mr. Hodges died there."

"Yes, I've heard that. I'm specifically interested in the orphans."

Total panic registered on her face. "It's dangerous snooping around asking about them," she said.

"I can take care of myself," he said. "Just show me the files, ma'am."

She jerked her bony shoulders upward as if he'd offended her, then escorted him to the microfiche section. He settled into the chair and pored over the clippings. First, he skimmed several articles about various supernatural sightings and legends. Apparently more than one person claimed they'd spotted the devil living in the woods. Other rumors told of a mutant species of people that had mountain lion heads. They fed on people. Pictures of the so-called creatures looked obscure in the shadows of the photographs. But they were creepy.

He read further, disgust shooting through him. Wild animals had been killed for ritualistic purposes at a nearby cliff and several people had died at a ridge they called Satan's Falls.

Finally he found an article about the orphanage. The caretakers, Hattie Mae and Howard Hodges, were supposedly dedicated to helping young girls in trouble. No names of the girls were listed, but they came from across the States. Many had been forced to be confined by the legal system, some were runaways, drug addicts, others homeless, pregnant teens. Girls no one wanted.

Like Elsie. Or so she'd thought.

He swallowed back sudden emotions, and tried to put an image of her out of his mind. With so many children in the center, especially pregnant teens, the orphanage must have offered medical care and counseling services. He'd explore that angle. Maybe a social worker or doctor could shed some light on Elsie and what had happened to her while she'd lived at the orphanage.

He flipped through several more articles, searching for names, and hit pay dirt. Local family practitioner Morty Mires had offered medical services while a counselor named Renee Leberman had assisted in the girls' placements.

He made a mental note to pay them both a visit.

Then he read on, noting various other articles about teenage crime that two girls from the orphanage had been blamed for. Again, no specific names were listed. Over the next three years, similar stories surfaced, along with articles about town protests and efforts to shut down the facility. Finally he located an article featuring the fire at Wildcat Manor.

Hattie Mae Hodges had called the police and firefighters who arrived in time to save most of the building. Barring two children who were unaccounted for, the others had survived. Elsie and a ten-year-old girl named Torrie, had been missing. Their bodies were never found, so police assumed they ran away.

Hattie Mae's husband, Howard, died in the fire, which started in the basement. The blaze was ruled accidental, although reports hinted at arson. The implication that the two missing girls had started the fire was clear.

Deke grimaced and scrubbed his hand over his face. Had the police searched for Elsie and the child, Torrie? Where had Elsie gone? Why had she run?

Because she was guilty….

If Elsie had set the fire that had caused Hodges's death, then she would have been charged with murder. That would explain why she'd fled Wildcat Manor and never returned. Only she'd come back now. And if the sheriff suspected her of arson or murder, why hadn't he questioned her or arrested her?

Why was he warning her to leave town instead of trying to pin the crime on her?

THREE HOURS LATER, Elsie finished her errands, and left the town square, the sight of two women and their little girls making her pause. She'd overheard the women, Donna and Eleanor, chatting in the store. Unable to help herself, she stood beside the soda shop and watched the children eating ice-cream cones and giggling. They were the same age as her daughter would have been.

"Come on, Missy, let's go to the park." Missy turned brown eyes toward her friend, a blue-eyed blond who reminded Elsie of someone, but the connection eluded her.

"We can ice-skate," Missy said. "Or do you want to swing, Ellen?"

Elsie choked back tears as they began to whisper. The mothers noticed Elsie and gave her an odd look, then bustled the girls away as if they thought Elsie was evil, just as the teenagers had done years ago. Choking back the pain in her chest, she headed to her car, the curious eyes of strangers burning her back. She checked over her shoulder sensing that someone in town had followed her, and saw a shadow disappear into an alley. Her nerves on edge, she thought about Deke and wished he was with her, but her last comment to him had probably sent him packing. It was better he left, she assured herself, although an emptiness swelled in her throat at the prospect of never seeing him again.

Twigs snapped behind her, and she glanced over her shoulder again, the certainty that she was being watched sending a chill up her spine. She hurried to her car, jumped in and locked the door, then scanned the street.

Nearly empty. Thank heavens.

Still, she checked over her shoulder as she drove up the winding road to the manor on the mountain. *Someone* had definitely been on her tail all day. Logging her every move. Waiting for their chance. When she was alone. Vulnerable.

Then they would strike.

Her palms grew sweaty as she gripped the steering wheel harder, fighting to keep the car on the road as the vicious wind whipped her sideways. The dark skies and ominous ridges reminded her that she skirted on the dangerous side simply by driving the curvy roads in treacherous weather conditions.

And that staying alone at Wildcat Manor posed other dangers, as well. Physical and mental.

The memories crashed, sharp and clawing at her sanity. The other children's faces. Girls so lost they cried into their pillows until dawn. Children having children, with no one to love them or care what happened. Men so despicable that they took from the innocent and laughed at the pain they caused.

People who stood by, watched and did nothing.

She had vowed all her life she would not be one of them.

But had she fallen into that trap by keeping silent? By not coming forward to expose the horrors that had taken place in the darkest hours of the night at the manor?

Her reputation and name be damned, what about the other girls? They were grown now with lives of their own. Even if she revealed the horrors at the orphanage, what would her announcement do to them? Some hopefully had survived, moved on to find families, husbands, lovers, happiness. They might not want her opening closed doors, their lives uprooted because guilt ate steadily at her conscience, like the mice that had nibbled away at the wooden floors in the rooms where the girls had slept.

Would exposing the truth somehow shatter any peace they'd found and destroy their lives?

Or would it help them in their personal recovery?

She had no right to make that decision for them. Besides, Hattie Mae and Howard Hodges were both dead. Who would believe her?

You've been in your own self-imposed prison anyway. What difference would it make if you came forward now?

No, God had punished her enough. She didn't

deserve to be put behind bars, caged like a wild animal....

Did she?

A tree limb flew across the road, and she jerked the car sideways to avoid it. Dead leaves and debris scattered before her, twigs snapping and breaking off the trees and falling to the icy ground as if they were nothing but toothpicks.

Her anxiety tripled as she veered onto the deserted drive that led up the hill to Wildcat Manor. The absence of a moon or stars painted the stone structure in abject darkness.

A fog of fear nearly engulfed her, but she summoned her courage. She'd purchased a small revolver to protect herself. If the man who'd attacked her appeared again, she'd be prepared.

She ground the car to a halt, tugging her coat around her as she gathered the gun to her side, then snatched two bags of groceries from the backseat. Shuffling them to one arm, she stumbled her way up the pebbled steps to the front door, her keys lodged between her numb fingers.

Suddenly, she stopped cold, her chest heaving at the sight on her front porch. The bloody carcass of a mountain lion lay on the doormat, its head severed. Blood also dotted the front windows and door. And the cryptic message warning her to leave was painted in bold, bloody letters.

You know what it's like to murder, Elsie. This could be you, next.

ELSIE TIMMONS.

God. He couldn't believe it. All these years he'd wondered what had happened to the little bitch, when she might reappear, where she'd been, if she'd resurface one day to destroy him….

Why had she returned now?

Was she looking for the lost girls? The sinners….

Anger, pure and bitter, snaked through him, coiling from deep in his belly as he fantasized about touching that long dark curly hair. Elsie, the girl who should have been grateful and compliant, the one who had balked and fought the hardest.

The one who had gotten away.

God, he had loved her feisty spirit. But Elsie wasn't innocent, either. She had secrets she didn't want exposed. Secrets she might die to protect.

Secrets he could use to destroy her.

A laugh bubbled in his throat and spilled out, echoing in the woods, its sound so filled with rage that animals skittered and ran to escape it.

Just as Elsie had.

But now she was back, she wouldn't escape him.

He'd make sure she never talked. Or if she did, that no one would believe her. They'd think she was crazy. They'd know what she had done.

And he'd make her suffer long and hard for it.

He lifted his hands, letting the blood spill down his fingers, remembering the joy he'd felt when he'd severed the animal's head.

The joy he'd feel when he did the same to Elsie.

Chapter Eight

Nausea climbed to Elsie's throat at the sight of the animal's brain matter spilling out, splattered against the door. The grocery bag slipped from her hands and hit the porch floor, contents overflowing. Suddenly, a firm hand gripped her arm. She screamed and jerked around, trying to raise the gun, but another hand grabbed it before she could raise the weapon.

"Elsie, it's me, Deke."

Her gaze shot upward, the scream on the tip of her tongue dying. "Deke?"

"Yes, you didn't hear me approach?"

She shook her head, glancing toward the driveway. His Range Rover was parked down the drive, but she should have heard his footsteps approaching. Yet he had walked so quietly she hadn't detected a sound.

Either that or she'd been in shock and had mentally blacked out for a moment.

He muttered an expletive as if he'd just seen the

mutilated mountain lion. "Damn it, what kind of sicko did this?" Releasing her, he eased her aside, putting himself between her and the nearly decapitated animal, another round of curses erupting from his mouth as he stared at the bloody message on the door. His anger forced her to take a step backward. When men lost their temper, they took it out on whoever was closest.

But he shocked her by kneeling to stroke the mountain lion's back, his tone lowering to a soothing pitch. "Poor fellow. You didn't have a chance, did you?"

Elsie's heart sputtered at Deke's tender reaction and the control he'd mastered over his anger. When she had been injured, he had touched her with the same kind of compassion, as if his fingers and gruff voice held magic.

"Did you see anyone?" he asked, teeth gritted.

"No. I just got here."

He glanced back up at her, pain in his eyes. What did he think about the message? Was he wondering who she'd killed?

"I'll bury him in the backyard," Deke said. "But first I want to check the house."

"I'll go with you."

"No." Steel hardened his tone this time. "Get in the car and lock the doors." His gaze fell to the revolver. "Do you know how to use that?"

She nodded, but didn't elaborate. More secrets she'd rather not confess. Yet the knowledge had saved her life a couple of times.

"If the guy who butchered this animal shows up, or comes near you, fire the gun." He tipped her chin up, then leaned forward and brushed a kiss across her lips. "Don't hesitate, Elsie. Whoever did this is one sick bastard."

She nodded, her lips tingling from his kiss, her mind memorizing his touch. She'd dealt with plenty of bastards over the years and knew how to fight. But she wasn't prepared for a man like Deke. The very reason she hadn't stopped him when he'd kissed her. She'd liked the feel of his lips, and the protective way he'd looked at her.

He removed a .38 from inside his jacket. "Now, go. He might be waiting inside."

She started to tell him she could take care of herself, that she had done so for years. But his lethal look forced her into silence, and she headed toward her car, scanning the woods beside her. She'd concede this point, only because Deke was here, and he was experienced, but she couldn't learn to rely on him.

And she couldn't let herself fall for him, no matter how tough or how gentle he acted. Or how well he kissed....

Besides, being near her put him in danger. She

didn't need another man's death on her conscience. And people wore masks. At first, they only revealed the layer on the outside, but peel it away, and ugliness lay below the surface.

Even as she thought it, her insides quivered with a protest. Deke was different.

She climbed in her car and locked the door, then braced the gun to fire as she watched the house. Drawing on self-preservation skills she'd learned on the streets, she yanked her cell phone from her purse and laid it on the seat beside her in case she needed to call for help. To the right of the manor, debris tumbled across the ice-coated land and pond, and the water shimmered with its own dark secrets. Hadn't she heard rumors that one of the girls claimed to have heard a baby crying out by the pond? The ghost of her own child, taunted to life by her guilt maybe? Or perhaps a little one who had drowned in the frigid water before Elsie had arrived.... Or Elsie's baby....

She jerked her attention back to the porch. Deke slowly entered the manor, his movements as sleek and smooth as a panther's, the scent of danger floating in the wind as the trees trembled around her.

She scanned the property again, then the outside of the house. A shadow of light flickered, and she glanced up at the attic dormer window. Darkness cloaked the stone structure, the windows mere black holes, but a movement caught her attention.

Her breath locked in her chest as a ghostly shape floated in front of the glass....

DEKE LISTENED FOR SIGNS of an intruder as he searched the dark corners and dusty closets of the manor, bracing himself for anything he might encounter—man or animal, or half human. His anger simmered inside like a fire that couldn't be extinguished. Whoever had killed the animal deserved to feel the same horrific pain he'd inflicted on the innocent cat. The fact that the man had used the brutality as a way to terrify Elsie was even more despicable.

Once he found the sicko, Deke would punish him. No animal or woman deserved such cruelty.

You know what it's like to murder.

A creaking sound from above jarred him, and he aimed his penlight to guide the way, utilizing his keen sense of vision and hearing. Every groan and rattle in the house made him pause. The dozens of nooks and crannies offered possible hiding places for the culprit that had to be checked out. Situated on top of the mountain, above the old mines that had been carved out of stone years ago when people migrated to the area looking for gold, tunnels might even run beneath the mountains. Back in Tin City, some builders had structured houses above or near the tunnels, providing secret escape routes in case of an emergency.

Convinced the main floor of the manor was empty, Deke climbed the steps to the second floor, hoping the intruder was waiting inside so he could confront him. He'd rub the man's face in the blood, make him choke on the smell of the vicious act he had committed by desecrating the wild animal, then torment him until he begged for his own life.

Shadows floated from the corners, while an odd scent of sandalwood and some odor he didn't quite recognize—maybe a chemical of some kind—engulfed him. The two dormlike rooms were empty, the bathrooms untouched, yet he sensed that someone had been inside the room where Elsie slept. He hadn't noted the details the first time he'd searched the house, and couldn't be sure. Not knowing everything she'd brought with her, meant she would have to check for missing items.

But the room was also empty.

The damn coward was sneaking in and out, playing games. Biding his time. Trying to rattle her.

Eventually, though, he would grow tired of the

game and he would surface. Then he might hurt Elsie.

Deke's jaw clenched. When he did, Deke would be waiting....

TENSION KNOTTED every muscle in Elsie's body as she waited on Deke's return. What kind of human would mutilate an animal and leave it on someone's doorstep?

Some crazy person from the mountains, someone who was homeless and so deranged he'd lost control of his senses?

No, this was personal. The intruder knew her. He had used *her* name in the warning. And he'd known that she had killed Hodges.

Seconds ticked by, excruciating in intensity as she waited for Deke to reappear. Finally, desperate to know if he was okay, she clutched the gun, preparing to leave the car and go inside. This battle was hers to fight, not Deke's.

Outside, an animal howled from the mountains, its shrill cry ringing in her ears, and she hesitated, the noises reminding her of the terrified cries of the girls who'd lived inside Wildcat Manor. The years fell away as if she'd lapsed into a time tunnel, taking her back. The images of the younger orphans, the loneliness and fear on their faces. The pregnant teens, scared for themselves, for their unborn babies. Then the newborns…taken away forever. The emptiness in the girls' eyes afterward.

Did the nightmares still haunt them? Did they still pine for their loved ones? The families they had lost, their innocence….

She reached for the door handle, determined to face those demons. She shouldn't have let Deke go in alone. She knew how to fight, how to shoot. She could watch his back.

The door clicked just as he emerged from the manor. He blinked, then strode toward her, his expression grim. She slid from the car, the gun in her hand. "Did you find anything?"

He shook his head, the wind tousling the dark strands of his hair across his brow. She had the insane urge to smooth the stray strands back in place. Not that his hair was neat, it was overly long, brushed his collar and looked as if he constantly ran his hands through it. Her gaze latched on to the worried look in his dark eyes. He was the most handsome man she'd ever known, and reminded her of a warrior from another time.

Except he was here, protecting her.

All because an older woman had asked him to.

That one detail told her he had honor.

"Elsie?"

"It's cold. Let's go inside," she whispered before she did something dangerous like kiss him. Except this time it wouldn't be a brush of lips, but an erotic, hungry kiss, filled with yearning.

"Are you sure you want to stay here tonight?" He gestured toward the porch. "We can go to a hotel."

Her nerves skittered in a thousand directions. An image of the two of them lying naked in a soft bed, safe, together, the sheets twisted around them, came to her, unbidden, but stirring desires. Their bodies entwined as lovers....

Yet, the shame of her past surfaced. Intruded on the image. The ugliness of her life here at the manor. And suddenly the thought of a man touching her repulsed her.

She backed away, casting her eyes away from him, toward the dark skies and tall mountain ridges. Her fingers felt numb, her heart even more empty. "I'm not going to run again. I did that before.... I won't this time."

"You mean when you ran away the night of the fire?"

Cold splintered through her. "I don't want to discuss the fire, Deke. Did you check the attic?"

"No, it was still locked from the outside."

"I saw a shadow up there while you were inside," Elsie said. "There may be someone hiding out upstairs."

His jaw tightened as he gestured toward the house. "Then let's check it out. If the guy who left that carcass is inside, there has to be another way to get in and out."

Elsie stepped forward, but he pushed her behind him. "Follow me. And keep that gun ready."

ELSIE'S UNWILLINGNESS to talk about the fire raised Deke's suspicions more. How the hell could he get her to trust him? She had been hurt by everyone she'd ever known, including her own family, the very people who should have loved and protected her. And no telling what had happened to her in that orphanage….

He slowly made his way up the steps again, this time his own nerves unsteady because Elsie was behind him. He wanted her safe, far away from this place.

"Do you have a key for the attic?" Deke asked.

Elsie nodded, retrieving her key chain from the pocket of her jeans where she'd stuffed it. She pointed to a small round key and Deke inserted it, then paused to listen. A creaking sound broke the quiet, then silence. He opened the door and entered the dark stairwell. A flapping sound echoed through the hollow spiral staircase, the scent of must and mildew wafting through the air.

The sound rippled through the silence again. An animal. Maybe trapped inside the attic.

Elsie startled and clutched his arm, tension vibrating in her fingers as she gripped him in the darkness.

"It's a bird," he said, hoping to calm her. "It probably built a nest here for the winter."

He scanned the murky interior with the penlight. A tall oval mirror occupied one corner, while an antique dresser, an open hand-painted wooden trunk full of children's toys and a couple of bags filled the opposite one.

"There's nobody here," Elsie whispered. "But I…know, I'm almost certain I saw a shadow a few minutes ago."

"Maybe a reflection from that mirror off the window," Deke suggested. He listened again, then inched his way behind the mirror. His jaw tightened when he spotted a red-headed falcon, its wing broken, its head twisted at an odd angle, lying in the corner. It looked weak, as if it had been there several days.

He glanced around the attic and noticed a hole near the window. Had the bird flown inside after it was injured, or had it gotten inside where an intruder harmed it?

He knelt and checked the falcon, talking in a low voice to comfort the wounded animal. Emotions choked his throat at the idea of losing another beloved wild creature.

"Is it going to be all right?" Elsie asked over his shoulder.

"I hope so. I'll try to nurse her back to health." Questions lingered in her eyes, ones he'd answer later. "Can you find me a blanket or something to wrap her in?"

Elsie nodded, then rushed over to one of the bags and returned a second later with an old faded bedspread. He gently wrapped the falcon in it, then stroked the crown of its head. "You're going to be all right. I promise I'll take care of you."

"Deke, how do you think the bird was injured?"

He shrugged, not wanting to alarm her more, but doubts already flickered in her expression. "I'm not sure."

Anxiety tightened her mouth. "Do you think the same person who killed that mountain lion might have harmed her?"

He had to be honest. "It's possible. I want to check for a secret door up here."

He stroked the bird one more time, promising to return, then stood and scanned the attic. On the far wall, a small door led to a crawl space. He pried open the door, while Elsie looked over his shoulder. "It looks like another storage area."

"Stay here," Deke said. "I'll see where it leads."

Elsie's face paled to a milky white. He hesitated, and gave her hand a squeeze, hating the fear in her eyes.

"Look around some more, see if you find anything that might indicate who's been here," he said. "I'll be right back."

She nodded, and he disappeared through the trapdoor, then followed it to the second floor where it emptied into the closet. Furious he hadn't noticed it before, he vowed to nail off the escape route tonight so the man couldn't come and go as he pleased.

Hating to leave Elsie alone long, he raced back up the steps to the attic. Her face had paled even more, and her body trembled. He narrowed his eyes, trying to discern if something else had happened to upset her.

In one hand, she clutched a small book to her chest. Curious, he inched toward her. She didn't seem to notice his approach. Instead she stood bone still, while she traced a finger over the edge of a wooden baby cradle. Tears clung to her long dark eyelashes, the sadness in her voice as she hummed a lullaby echoing in the silence....

ELSIE SLOWLY RAN her finger along the cradle, caressing the smooth blond wood, gently pushing it back and forth, a lullaby humming in her head. "Twinkle, twinkle, little star, how I wonder what you are."

Her mother's soft melodic voice had calmed Elsie at night, even when she'd grown past the age where she should have been listening to lullabies.

Another baby's cry squealed in her head, this one terrified at being handed to a stranger. The girl who'd birthed him sobbed into her pillow, battling the truth that she couldn't take care of herself, much less the baby. But her despair was painful to watch.

Jan. She had taught Elsie about shattered innocence. The one that had struck Elsie the hardest because Elsie had never before witnessed childbirth, not until she watched Jan deliver her five-pound son. Elsie hadn't known the pain of delivery or the agony of watching a baby being torn from its mother's arms, either.

Yet she had empathized with mother and child. Because she'd only been four when her daddy had taken her from her own mother. At least the baby wouldn't know…or would it?

Elsie had certainly never forgotten. And she'd known the emptiness of thinking that her mother hadn't wanted her.

The question had haunted her—one day Jan's baby would find out she'd given him away. Then he would suffer. And he'd probably hate her.

After that, there had been others. So many others. Some girls had handled delivery and signing away their child with utter acceptance, hoping to escape their shameful, unwed pregnancy and build a life for themselves, glad to be rid of the unwanted baby that would bind them together forever and limit them from reaching their own potential. They had called the child a burden. They were young. They could have another kid when they were ready.

A few were conflicted in other ways. Smart enough to realize the limitations of their age and financial situation yet not as callous. They believed wholeheartedly that they were doing the best thing for the child by placing it in a home with two loving parents. They had shed tears, but their pain had been mingled with hope and prayers and a sacrifice born of love.

Others had crumbled under the shame and emptiness. Had never recovered from the bleakness of knowing that they had given away a child as if it were nothing but a meaningless possession.

For Elsie, it had been different. Her choice had been stripped from her. But the pain had been just as horrific. She'd felt as if someone had literally carved a hole in her flesh with a knife.

"Elsie?" Deke's quiet, gruff voice broke through her trip down memory lane.

"What's wrong?" Deke asked quietly.

She swallowed back the anguish she'd lived with for so long, and faced him, tearless, determined to keep her secret buried next to her heart where her baby still lay. "My mother used to sing lullabies to me at night." She managed a small smile. "I guess that's silly, but I was so small when I left, that I'd forgotten that until now."

He jammed his hands in his pockets. "I can understand that. I…when my father was arrested, I was only a kid, too. But he had the deepest voice, and the widest hands, the longest fingers. Those hands were so strong, I used to watch him chop wood and build furniture with them, then he'd use those same hands to soothe the injured birds." Deke's voice sounded thick, as if he thought he'd revealed too much. "I wanted to be just like him."

"You knew he couldn't have murdered Hailey's family, didn't you?"

He nodded.

"Oh, Deke, you must have been so angry and hurt."

He gave her a steady look, but emotions flickered in his eyes. Emotions he tried to hide just as she tried to hide hers. "I was. Rex, our oldest brother, he took care of everyone. Mother. Me and Brack." He chuckled, but bitterness laced the sound.

"The two of us were so little we didn't understand. For the first month, I thought my dad would walk back home any minute. Then the truth hit me, and I hated everyone around me for not helping him. The people in town ridiculed us, forced us to move away. The kids taunted my brothers and me, calling us a killer's son." He hesitated, met her gaze. "But your mother stood beside mine," Deke said. "Deanna was a true friend, the only one brave enough to stand up for us against the town. For that, my family will forever be grateful."

The connection between them was filled with tension, unanswered questions, pain, the memory of her mother. God, she wanted to know her again, to see the loving woman Deke talked about, to feel her arms around her.

But there was more. She wanted to comfort Deke now. He had suffered as a child. Had felt deserted. Lost. But he hadn't folded. And although he was tough, muscular, commanding, he possessed compassion and a tenderness she'd craved all her life.

Elsie started forward, but he held a hand up in warning. "It was a long time ago, Elsie. My family's back now, I'm trying to let the anger go."

"Letting the past go, it's not easy," Elsie said softly.

"No, but that's why I want to help you and your mother reunite."

His gaze locked with hers, and she sensed he was waiting for her to offer more. But the cradle drew her eye again, and she clammed up. She couldn't talk about the cradle, the baby….

A heartbeat lapsed before he spoke, but his eyes held disappointment that she didn't trust him. "What's in your hand?"

She clutched the book to her chest. "Hattie Mae's diary. I…I thought if I read it, it might help me understand her a little better." She pointed to the trapdoor. "Did you find out where that crawl space leads?"

"To the closet in one of the dorm rooms. I'll seal it and that window so no one can use it again."

He closed the distance between them, and stroked her cheek with his hand. "Elsie, I told you about my father. Now tell me about the fire that night. About you and Torrie."

"What do you know about Torrie, and that night?"

"Just what the papers said," he murmured. "That the police called it an accident. That Hattie Mae phoned the fire house, and they rescued all of the girls, except for you and Torrie. What happened to her?"

Elsie rubbed a hand over her eyes, blinking back tears. "I don't know."

Deke gripped her arm and forced her to look at him. "Tell me, Elsie. Did Hodges hurt Torrie? Was he abusing her? And you and the other girls?"

"Torrie," she whispered, tears filling her eyes. "That night he took her to the basement. He was going to hurt her. I had to get her away."

His grip loosened, his fingers tenderly stroking the place where he'd held her. "What was he doing to her?"

"He…it doesn't matter now. He's dead and she's safe."

"How do you know that?"

"I helped her escape. Then we found a church and the priest took her in."

"He took you in, as well, then?"

"No." Terror gripped her. "I ran. I…I wanted to go back and save the other girls. But the police were there, already asking questions."

"About the fire?"

She nodded. "And they were talking about taking the girls away, moving them, so I thought they'd be better off away from Wildcat Manor."

Deke's steady gaze focused on her face. His dark intense look burned her down to her soul, as if he already knew the answers. "What caused the fire, Elsie? Did you set it?"

How could she describe what had happened and not reveal everything?

You know what it's like to murder.

"I don't want to talk about this anymore." She ran toward the steps, but he caught her again, imploring her with his dark enigmatic eyes.

"I thought you said you weren't running anymore." He cupped her face in his palms. "Then why are you running from me, Elsie? I'm trying to help. Just trust me."

Chills rippled through Elsie. "Don't you get it,

Deke? I can't trust anyone." Tears stung her eyes as she hurried down the steps.

Like the wild animals who hid behind the shadows of the trees and boulders in the mountains, she was safer in her solitude. There, no one could hurt her. No one could see her sorrow.

Afraid she couldn't contain her emotions any longer, she moved to lock herself in the bedroom. Maybe she'd read Hattie Mae's journal. Maybe she'd find answers there, the truth, and then she could find forgiveness.

But she froze in the doorway of the bedroom, a sick feeling overwhelming her. At the foot of the bed lay a baby blanket just like the one she'd slept with as a child. The one she'd left here at Wildcat Manor the day she'd escaped.

The one she'd wanted to wrap her own child in some day.

But she'd lost the baby girl and left her buried here at the manor.

Chapter Nine

Deke had no idea whether he should follow Elsie and make her talk or give her space. He felt raw inside, had shared more about himself than he'd ever revealed to another human, especially a woman.

But she'd turned away anyway.

Knowing she was hiding inside that bedroom with the door locked, he allowed his own anger over the brutal animal slayings to fester. First, he had to attend to the falcon. He pulled on gloves, then carefully cradled the bird into his arms. Her breathing had grown shallow. He stroked the crest of the falcon's head, speaking in the low voice he used to communicate with the birds of prey. Seconds later, the bird twitched slightly against him, then relaxed, cocking her head as if she understood.

Finally, he went outside to the toolshed, and let her rest beside him while he built a cage. He continued to calm her as he hammered the strips of wood together and attached screen meshing for sides. Satisfied with the product, he placed the blanket and bird inside, then left fresh water, and promised he'd return to check on her progress.

Back at the house, he carried the groceries in and put them away, then placed the dead mountain lion on another old blanket. He cleaned the blood off the porch and door, grabbed a shovel from the toolshed and hiked toward the woods, cradling the mutilated cat as if it was a child. A few feet inside the dense snow-laden branches, he found a dry spot, safeguarded somewhat from the wilder animal life that lived deeper in the woods.

Another winter storm threatened, so he hurried to dig a deep hole, placed the lion inside and covered it with dirt. To mark and protect the grave, he gathered several large stones and placed them over the mound.

When he finished, he studied the gray mottled sky, anxious about the danger following Elsie. Agitation tightening his muscles, he strode back to the house, hoping Elsie had surfaced, but she remained locked away in that bedroom. Still angry, he went and boarded up the secret passage.

Satisfied, he punched in Rex's number to update him, his mind warring with what to tell his brother. He still had nothing definitive on the person threatening Elsie. Nothing that he could use to end the case and convince her to return to Tin City.

He had to work harder, dig deeper into the past. Push Elsie.

Rex's voice echoed over the line. "Deke, good to hear from you."

"I'm not sure you'll say that after we talk."

"Why? What's wrong?"

"Elsie won't budge. Something bad happened in that orphanage a few years ago, Rex, Something that traumatized her. She doesn't trust anyone, especially me."

"You or men in general?"

"I can't be sure. The minute I start to get close to her, and I think she'll talk, she runs like a scared kitten."

"Damn. I can't tell Deanna that. It will crush her."

"I know." Deke filled him in on the last twenty-four hours, then focused on the details of the past he'd learned from Elsie. "Apparently, old man Hodges abused the kids. One night, Elsie caught him with a girl named Torrie and helped her escape. She claims she left her at a church, then, well, hell, she didn't say any more. But I think she set the fire that killed Hodges."

"Geez. Have the police been looking for her?"

"The report listed the fire as accidental." Deke paused. "It gets worse, Rex. Today someone pushed Elsie into the street, and a truck nearly ran her over."

Rex muttered a curse beneath his breath. "Is she all right?"

"Yeah, but she was shaken." Hell, so was he, more than he wanted to admit. But he couldn't let himself go soft. Then he'd be no good at his job. "The sheriff questioned her afterward, and warned her to leave town."

"Did he mention the fire?"

"No, and that struck me as odd. Even some of the news clippings I read insinuated that arson was involved. I can't figure out why they didn't try to find the person who set the fire. If it was Elsie, why wouldn't he have mentioned it today?"

"Maybe he knew what was going on at the orphanage," Rex suggested.

Deke's blood ran cold. That was a distinct possibility, and could be the reason he didn't want Elsie around. And if the sheriff had known, others might have, too.

But if they were aware of the abuse, why didn't someone help those poor children? What kind of cruel and inhuman people lived in Wildcat?

Rex cleared his throat. "If Hodges was abusing the girls, Deke, Elsie could have pleaded self-defense," Rex said. "She was only a child."

He sensed Elsie had never known the joys of childhood, or what it was like to have someone take care of her and protect her.

Damn it. He shouldn't care. The last time he had, a woman had used him. He'd tried to protect her kid, too, then the woman had turned on him.

"I know that, and so do you," Deke said in a gruff voice. "But she was a terrified girl. I don't know for sure if Hodges abused her, but I suspect he did. And if the sheriff knew and kept silent, how could she go to him?"

"That's true." Rex cursed again, and Deke's pulse quickened. Elsie must have felt utterly alone and abandoned. His own childhood pain suddenly didn't seem as harsh—after all, he and his brothers had had each other, and a mother who loved them.

"I don't understand why she won't return to Falcon Ridge with you," Rex said. "If she was abused in that orphanage, why stay there?"

Deke ran a hand through his hair. "After she left Torrie at a church, she went back to save the other girls, but the police were already there. She plans to build the teen center to make amends, then she'll face Deanna."

"Blow the lid on them, Deke, then bring her home. Her mama will be waiting."

Emotions clogged Deke's throat. Yes, Deanna would. Just as his mother had waited for his father.

As he hung up, his chest heaved. Elsie's haunted dark brown eyes taunted him. She thought he would judge her for her past. But there was nothing she could tell him to make him look down upon her.

Not when her suffering ate at his soul.

Damn it, he was losing control. He would not get involved.

After all, what kind of promises could he make? A few hours? A week. A month maybe? What could he say? He was attracted to her? He wanted her physically?

Hell, he did want Elsie. Physically his body burned for her, his arms craved her, his mouth longed to touch hers. And he wanted to be inside her, giving her pleasure.

But could he offer more than that?

He scrubbed his hand over his beard stubble, a reminder of the hellion he'd been as a teen, the hard-edged private investigator and rough falconer he had become.

Commitment to anything besides the falcons and his job had never been an issue. But he could not walk away from Elsie until he convinced her she was a beautiful, desirable woman. That she was worthy of love regardless of the demons chasing her.

He clutched the stair rail with sweaty hands, the memory of the dead animal a reminder of the violence and evil here. No, he wouldn't leave Elsie or any woman to face this kind of monster.

ELSIE STROKED THE EDGE of the faded yellow blanket, memories bombarding her. The night her father had taken her from Tin City, she'd clung to the childhood keepsake. It had been the only thing familiar to her in a world that had suddenly been turned upside down. Besides, her mother had made it for her. Every time she ran her fingers over her name embroidered in the fine thread, she imagined her mother's fingers sewing the tiny stitches, humming in that soft voice that had always soothed Elsie's bad dreams.

Her father had ridiculed her about holding on to the security blanket. She had tried to let it go, but at night, she'd dig it out from the closet and hug it while she slept. And when he'd taken her to Wildcat Manor, she'd hidden it inside her pillowcase.

Tears trickled down her cheeks. During her pregnancy, she'd vowed to give it to her own baby. But she had failed her baby and she had died at birth. The horror still swept over her in unexpected waves every time she saw an infant in a stroller or its mother's arms.

If she hadn't been a bad girl, if she hadn't been so stupid to trust that the people at the orphanage would help her, her daughter might have survived.

Then she would have a ten-year-old little girl now. Just like Donna and Eleanor.

Whoever left the blanket on the bed had known her dark, ugly secrets.

She made mental notes of all the people with knowledge of her pregnancy—her father, Hattie Mae, Mr. Hodges, the doctor in town who'd provided the girls' health care and the lawyer who'd arranged the adoptions. Of course she hadn't needed his legal services in the end, but they had forced her to meet with him to discuss her options. All the young girls had been encouraged to give up their babies. Elsie had insisted that she wanted to keep her child, that her baby needed her. And truthfully, she had needed it.

The dark reddish-brown stain on the blanket practically pulsed with life, reminding her of death and the blood she'd lost in childbirth. Who had kept her blanket all these years?

Hattie Mae? If so, who had gotten it after her death? And who had placed it at the foot of her bed?

Doctor Mires or Mr. Thompson? They both had reasons not to want the truth about Wildcat Manor revealed. Would they hurt her to force her into silence?

She had to look into their eyes and confront them.

Deke's expertise would help. But then she would have to explain everything....

No, she couldn't do that. She'd confront the two men on her own tomorrow, and find out exactly what they knew. Then she'd make it clear that she had no intention of being scared away.

And if they started tossing around warnings—she'd toss one right back. If she had to, she'd swallow her pride, go public about Hodges, about the abuse and the adoptions....

DEKE TOOK A QUICK SHOWER to wash the scent of blood and death off him, then checked on Elsie. The door remained closed, and he almost knocked, but instinct forced him to back away. He wanted Elsie to trust him enough to come to him on her own.

Rain splattered the windows and wind thrashed hail against the stone house, the haze of fog and more dark clouds evident through the window as he descended the steps.

Apparently, the power had been restored while Elsie was in town. She'd bought a large piece of fish, along with a box of rice, so he quickly marinated the fish, prepared a salad out of the veggies, cooked the rice, then seared the salmon in a pan. Living on his own, he had learned a few culinary skills, most of which involved grilling, but the manor didn't have the luxury of a grill. A large overgrown garden that had perhaps held herbs or flowers at one time surrounded a large stone patio off the French doors. The garden had possibilities for revival, but now the thick tangle of vines and overgrown brush looked sinister, as if it might provide a hiding place for someone watching the manor. He bolted the door, vowing silently to check it out later.

Satisfied with the meal, he walked up the stairs and knocked on Elsie's door. "Elsie, I made dinner. Will you please come down and eat?"

Something rustled inside, then Elsie's low voice reverberated through the doorway. "Go away, Deke. I need to be alone."

He ground his teeth. "I'm not leaving, not after what happened today in town, and especially not after that warning when you got home." God, she had to be rational. "Please, come out. You have to be hungry."

Slowly the door opened. Her eyes looked red rimmed as if she'd been crying, but he refrained from comment.

"You don't need to stay now, Deke. I'm safe. I'll lock the house and be all right."

"I told you I'm not leaving." He reached for her hand, but she stiffened, and he took a step back from the door, not conceding, but offering her breathing space.

"It's just dinner, Elsie," he said softly. "I'm not going to hurt you, I promise."

Her wary look spoke volumes, but she bit her lip

and stepped into the hallway. When they entered the kitchen, surprise flickered across her face at the sight of the fire he'd built, and then again at the table. A second later, distrust swam in her eyes as she turned to face him.

"Is something wrong?" he asked.

She swallowed, drawing his attention to the fine column of her neck, to the tender skin he suddenly wanted to kiss.

"Just dinner?"

Pain darkened her expression. He glanced at the wine and candlelight and realized it painted a seductive picture. "Just dinner." He held up his hands in a peace gesture. "I promise. I won't touch you if you don't want me to."

She clenched the napkin in a shaky hand, but sat down at the table. "I'm sorry, Deke. But no man has ever cooked for me. I…can't seem to figure out why you're so persistent."

"I told you this afternoon. Deanna is a friend of the family. And you can be, too, if you'll just trust me."

She clamped her teeth over her lip, but remained silent, her other hand reaching out to grab her glass and sip her water.

He gestured toward the wine. "Would you like a glass? I thought it might relax you."

She nodded. "We could probably both use one."

"You're right. It's been a tough day." He uncorked the bottle, then poured them both a glass and joined her at the table. His leg brushed hers as he tried to fit his long limbs into the chair. Relief flooded him when she didn't pull away.

The conversation lagged, tension humming between them as she nibbled at her food. He devoured his, trying to forget the case. But forgetting the case meant his mind was free to wonder about other things. Like how the skin at the nape of her neck would taste. How her lips would feel against his a second time. How she might respond to his touch. How her naked body would feel tucked against his own.

Her gaze met his and heat spiraled between them. He tugged his shirt collar open slightly, wishing he hadn't built the fire or that he'd left the damn door open. She studied him for a long moment, pain etched on her face.

"I promise you, Elsie, I won't hurt you."

"I almost believe you," she said softly.

His heart sputtered. He gently reached out and laid his hand over her trembling one. "I don't know what kind of men you've known, but I would never do anything you didn't want me to."

A moment of naked longing registered in her eyes, robbing his breath. She wanted him to kiss her.

Desire flooded her eyes, and she parted her lips slightly, the rosy hue drawing his gaze to her mouth.

Dear God…what should he do? He'd vowed to go slowly, yet here she was practically offering.

Instead, he drank his wine greedily, trying to fill his hunger another way. He couldn't afford to allow himself to pursue this…need pulsing between him and Elsie. That would be taking advantage of Elsie.

But she twined her slender fingers around the stem of the glass and took a sip of the merlot, her gaze still fixed on his, then dropping to his mouth.

His resistance teetered. Her close call with death today triggered a longing that he'd never expected to feel. Images of her winding her fingers around his neck, then tracing them over his bare chest and lower to stroke his belly, then his aching sex, taunted him.

He couldn't pursue it, though, and frighten her off.

"Thank you, Deke. The dinner was wonderful."

He dotted his napkin across his sweating forehead. "I'm glad you enjoyed it."

Again, tension sizzled in the air between them. Eyes locked. She licked her lips.

"Are you only being nice to me because you think you owe my mother?" she asked softly.

Her blunt comment took him off guard. "I…at first, that was the reason."

"And now?"

Wariness darkened her eyes, but desire also

flickered in the depths. He didn't quite know how to answer.

"Now…" He hesitated, hating the churning in his stomach. "Now I want to protect you."

Disappointment tightened her mouth. "Because you think I'm helpless?" Anger tinged her voice. "Well, I'm not, Deke. I know how to fight, how to take care of myself, how to shoot that gun. And I won't hesitate to do it."

"That doesn't mean you have to face everything alone all the time, Elsie."

Emotions clouded her eyes. "I don't know any other way."

He twined her fingers in his own, stroking her palm with his other hand as he pulled her hand into his lap. "Let me show you."

Her gaze swung to his, and he read the questions, the uncertainty. She wanted to believe him, but she had no family, no one to relate to. No one who would give their life for her as he and his brothers would for their family.

No wonder she was so wary and distrustful.

The touch of her skin sent fire through him, and he traced his fingers over her hand, allowing her time to learn his touch. Hopefully, one day she wouldn't turn away or resist him if he asked for more.

"I wish I could change the past for you," he said in a low voice. "But I won't desert you like everyone else did." His heart pounded. "Deanna didn't abandon you of her own free will, either, just as my father didn't me."

He heard his own words, and some of the bitterness and anger he'd held on to for years faded away. It was time to let it go. Move on. Enjoy the future with his family. He could only do that through forgiveness and acceptance.

Just as Elsie would have to do one day.

"I know," Elsie whispered. "I do want to see her, Deke. So badly. You can't even begin to imagine."

She lowered her head, but he tipped her face up with his thumb. "Tell me, Elsie, maybe I can help."

"When I do," she said softly, "I want to be whole. I want her to be proud of me."

God, he wanted to make love to her. "She will be proud of you no matter what you do, or what happened in the past."

Her chin trembled. "I...wish I could believe that."

"Then let's leave here. I'll prove it to you, and so will your mother."

Pain tightened her face into a haunted expression. "Don't you see? I can't move on without closing the door to my past. And I have to rectify the wrong that was done here."

He spoke without even thinking, "Did you ever think that just by shutting down the orphanage, you helped? That the girls were better off because you were brave enough to run?" His voice rose in conviction. "Maybe they were sent back to their families or to a better place with caring people. At least they were free of Hodges and this damned town."

"But I can't know that."

He knew all about guilt. The power it had to trap you. If she wanted this center to help others, how could he deny her?

He brushed her cheek with the pad of this thumb. "Then we'll find out together."

Elsie's shocked look brought him to a standing position. Hope lit her eyes, making her even more beautiful. He wanted to erase the anguish in her eyes.

He circled in front of the table and bent to cradle her face in his hands. The desire inside him roared her name, and he answered by pressing his lips to hers. First gently. When she met his lips with a soft purr, he deepened the kiss, twirling his tongue across her lips repeatedly, gently at first, then as his need grew, more forcefully until she opened her mouth and let him inside. He savored her sweet taste, the silent moment of trust. He tunneled his hands into her hair, angling his head to the side as he lowered his mouth to nip at her neck. "You are so beautiful, Elsie. So sweet and caring."

She moaned and spread her hands on his chest. He hesitated, thinking she meant to pull away, yet she pressed one hand to his cheek, tilting her head back in submission. The simple gesture took his breath away. He nibbled at her ear, then ran his tongue down her throat until she sighed and slid her arms around his neck. Taking her signal as one of pleasure, he dipped his head lower to tease the soft skin at the curve of her breasts. Raw hunger drove him, and he lowered one hand to gently touch her breast, so delicately at first that he didn't think she felt it. His own need mounting, he found her mouth again and kissed her with his entire being, squeezing her plump breast into his hand as she clung to him. Even through her sweater, the budding tip of her nipple hardened. His sex pulsed against his jeans, and he spread his thighs and captured her in the V, her sex pressed against his. She froze slightly, and he realized he'd gone too far. Had been selfish. Needy.

He reined in his desire, fought for control and gently eased back. Desire simmered in her eyes. Her face was flushed, her lips parted, her breathing erratic.

But a sliver of fear also flickered in the depths of her eyes, and guilt slammed into him.

"I didn't mean to frighten you," he said softly.

Her breath hitched. "I…you didn't."

He threaded his fingers through her hair again. "Then what is it?"

She lowered her head against his chest, her voice

quavering, "I can't do this, Deke. I'm sorry, I just can't…finish."

He eased a strand of her delicate curly hair behind one ear. "I'm sorry I pushed. But Elsie, I'm not sorry I kissed you."

"Deke, it's not that…I do want you, but—"

"Shh." He brushed his lips across hers, softly, gently. "It's all right, Elsie." He kissed her forehead again, just a brush of his lips. "If we are ever together, it will be when you're ready."

Knowing that if he didn't leave her that minute, he might kiss her again, he released her. He had to be alone, commune with the animals.

"Lock the door," he said in a gruff voice. "And keep the gun beside you."

"Where are you going?" she asked softly.

"Don't worry. I'll be back." With a half smile, he left her to think about what he'd said.

He had to regroup.

But he wouldn't go far. Because he meant what he'd said. He wouldn't desert her. And he'd prove to her that all men weren't vile, that not all men hurt women.

That some men not only took pleasure, but they gave it, as well.

ELSIE PRESSED A FINGER to her lips, her skin still tingling with erotic sensations from Deke's kiss. He had been so tender yet seductive. Had stirred desires that she'd never expected to feel again. A hunger that had nearly driven her wild, straight into his arms without even thinking about the consequences.

She hugged her arms to herself. He made her ache and burn for his touch. For more. For him to make love to her.

But Hattie's words haunted her, "Physical pleasure is wrong, girls. It's sinful."

Elsie had paid a harsh price for her first experience in lovemaking. Only with Deke, she was older…could things possibly be different? Would she ever be able to have a normal relationship with a man?

No. Not after her past….

Not with all the bitterness, fear and guilt that had eaten at her soul for the past decade.

Yet as tender as Deke had been, his hunger had been palpable. Completely male. Guarded but potent. Asking and giving.

She didn't know how to accept that kind of sexual interchange. In the past, she'd only known roughness. That she was expected to give. That when it was over, she had felt empty.

Now, her insides quivered with the need to feel his touch again. A warm unsettled feeling throbbed deep within her. How could Deke make her feel this way when other men's touches had turned her stomach? And what would happen if she actually encouraged him? Would she freak out and run away as she had with the last guy who'd tried to get close to her? Would she be able to please him the way a man wanted?

Doubt and uncertainty clouded the euphoria his touch had evoked. Irritated with herself, she poured another glass of wine, then retreated to her room, alone, where she was safe with her secrets.

The baby blanket mocked her from the dresser, and anger flooded her. She couldn't show this to Deke, but she couldn't throw it away, either. She had to know who had left it for her.

Hands trembling, she folded it and hid it beneath her bag, then spotted Hattie Mae's diary. Would she be violating the woman's privacy if she read it? Probably.

Then again, if Hattie Mae had revealed something about the adoptions or the other girls in the diary, she had to read it.

The creaking sound of the cradle from the attic echoed in her ears, a haunting sound that had repeatedly grated on her conscience in her nightmares. Driven by the painful sound, she opened the journal and began to read.

THE SOFT CREAK, creak, creak of the rocking chair calmed Eleanor Cross's nerves as she rocked her infant daughter back and forth, soothing the bubbles from her stomach as she patted her back. God, how she loved this little girl.

Her other daughter's voice humming from her bedroom while she played with her Barbie dolls drifted through the room, and she smiled again. Missy was such a special child. An angel. The first of her children.

The one who had filled the endless void in her life when she'd been informed she couldn't bear children.

Then her brother, Morty, had spoken with her in private and suggested adoption. At the time, her husband had run off, so her chances had been slim.

Three months later, only minutes after birth, Missy had been placed in her arms. She owed her brother dearly.

Never far away, the ten-year-old stepped inside the nursery wearing Barbie pajamas, a wide smile on her face. Always exuberant and bustling with energy, she rushed inside and planted a big kiss on her new little sister's cheek, then on Eleanor's.

"Night, little Dorrie. Night, Mommy."

"Good night, princess."

Missy skipped from the room hugging her Harry Potter book to her chest, her long black hair swinging from side to side. Eleanor's heart skipped a beat. She had been so lucky to have been given two beautiful girls. She'd do anything in the world to protect them.

Panic suddenly stole her joy as she recalled the gossip about Elsie Timmons's return. She bit down on her tongue to stifle a cry, determined not to startle the infant in her arms.

No, Dorrie was safe.

It was Missy she had to worry about. Missy with the smile that went on forever, and the heart of an angel.

Her brother had warned her to keep the adoption secret. And she had. But if the Timmons woman poked around too much or stirred up trouble over the adoptions, he and Burt Thompson might be placed under scrutiny by the authorities. And if they broke or decided to come clean…

No, that could not happen.

She wished that she'd asked the name of Missy's birth mother, but at the time she hadn't wanted to know. Now, the urge was driving her insane with worry.

Cradling the baby in her arms, she laid her in the crib, then hurried to her bedroom, shut the door and phoned her brother.

Seconds later, his answering machine kicked in. Damn it. She left a message, then phoned Thompson, pacing the white carpet as she waited. He answered on the third ring, his voice agitated. "I told you not to call me at home."

"Listen, Burt, I have to know who Missy's birth mother is so I can protect her."

"I can't divulge that information, and you know it."

"But I heard one of the girls from the orphanage is back." Hysteria rattled her voice. "What if she's looking for her baby?"

"We'll handle her," Thompson snapped. "Just stay calm."

"How can I be calm when that tramp is in town? Even if she's not Missy's mother, if she opens up about the adoptions, then other girls might come forward." A shudder coursed through her. "I can't lose Missy, Burt, you know that." She heaved, barely able to breathe. "I just can't. I would die without her."

"You won't lose her," Thompson promised. "Trust me, Mires and I will keep the Timmons girl from talking."

Eleanor inhaled a calming breath as she hung up, but the lawyer had not assuaged her anxiety. Instead her imagination created a whirlwind of possible scenarios. She'd never attended college like Morty, but she wasn't ignorant, either. She'd read about lawsuits pertaining to adoptions, the birth mother's rights, some adopted children even being given the option of meeting the birth mother, then choosing who they wanted to live with.

And she had a history. If the courts got hold of it, they'd make her look irresponsible....

Another possibility stabbed at her insides. What if her brother or Thompson decided to tell their secrets? Thompson was such a money-hungry bastard that he'd probably keep his mouth shut. But Morty—he was a good man. The little tramps hadn't deserved to keep those infants. But her brother had taken care of those troubled teens and helped them find homes for their unwanted babies out of the goodness of his heart.

What if he released the list of adopting parents to the police? What if he talked to Elsie? Just how much did the girl know?

Her chest tight, she went to her oldest daughter's bedroom and stared at her while she slept. Fierce protective instincts brought tears to her eyes, and she had to touch Missy's cheek just to reassure herself that she was still there, not an apparition.

No one would take her beloved little girl from her.

If she had to, she'd kill anyone who tried to jeopardize their relationship. Then she'd take Missy and Dorrie and disappear forever….

Chapter Ten

Elsie's skin crawled as she read Hattie Mae's journal.

November 1
Today Howard asked me to marry him. I was so
excited. I know my family thinks I'm too young,
but I love him with all my heart, and I know
we'll be happy together. I'm already dreaming
of having a family with him. That's all I've ever
wanted—a husband and children of my own.

Elsie's heart squeezed. She couldn't imagine
Hattie Mae young and in love. All she remembered
was the cowering, frightened woman who obeyed
her husband's commands. Although later, when he
wasn't around, she had occasionally slipped in to
see the girls at night with soothing words and a sad,
almost apologetic smile.

She skimmed farther, and found the first thirty
pages consisted of similar entries—Hattie Mae

and Howard were in love. They bought a small house. They were trying to conceive.

Farther in, the entries became darker, filled with sadness, frustration and a deep sense of guilt.

December 24
I had hoped today I'd find out that I was with child, but once again, I failed. Howard looks at me differently now, as if he can barely stand to touch me, as if I'm tainted because I haven't conceived. He found me crying when he got home from work, and he slapped me and told me to stop behaving like a child.

But I smelled perfume on him, and I think he'd been with someone else. Maybe someone who is more woman than me....

Midway through the book, the abuse had grown rampant, both verbally and physically.

April 10
Howard called me "barren" today. I pleaded with him to understand, told him I would go to the doctor for more tests, but he said he doesn't want me that way anymore. All I am to him is a maid and housekeeper. Even then, he criticizes my cooking. The meat is never done enough, the vegetables are soggy. And

then he complains about my cleaning. There's dust on the sideboard, the towels in the bathroom aren't hung evenly.

I wish I could just fade away. I don't deserve to live....

Elsie brushed a tear from her eye. She'd never understood how Hattie Mae had stood by and watched her husband hurt the girls, but now she did. Hattie Mae had been beaten down long before any of the teenagers had come along.

She flipped through several pages and discovered entries about the orphanage.

August 13
I spoke with the pastor in town, and he suggested that I must accept my fate as a childless woman, and find a purpose for my life. He said a social worker from Nashville planned to set up a home for orphaned kids and pregnant teenagers in Wildcat Manor.

Howard is out of work and we haven't been able to pay our bills lately. I wonder what he'll think if I offer to go to work at the orphanage. I'm almost afraid to tell him.

September 30
Reverend Alter phoned today and offered a caretaker position to me and Howard. He says

we can live free at the manor if we oversee the place and the kids. I told Howard, and he stormed out the door. He said he didn't need charity and didn't want anything to do with sinful brats.

October 21
They turned off the power today and Howard gave in. We moved into the manor. Renee Leberman, the social worker, brought two little girls today. One is eight, the other five. They're so precious. Although they're frightened, I know they need me. The sound of laughter and children in the house will be good for me and Howard.

Elsie bit back a sarcastic, bitter comment. At least Hattie Mae had had good intentions, and hopes when she'd started the center.

Curious to know when things changed, she continued to read.

January 11
Oh my God. Howard hasn't slept with me in a year now, but tonight…I can't believe what I thought I heard. He went into one of the girls' rooms. I prayed he was softening toward them, and he said he would turn out the

lights for me, but he stayed in there a long time. And when he came out, I slipped down the hall and heard ten-year-old Joan crying. I went into her room, but she hid her face in the pillow and refused to talk to me.

February 18
The nights are almost unbearable now. I told Howard to stay out of the girls' rooms, but he beat me senseless and locked me inside my room in the dark. He said it was my fault because I couldn't satisfy him.

March 1
Today one of the girls gave birth, a difficult one, and we almost lost her. Then she changed her mind about giving up her baby and Howard got ugly....

I don't know how I can let things continue. But at night, Howard beats me religiously and locks me in my room. If I tell anyone, he'll kill me.

Then what will happen to the girls?

Elsie couldn't read any farther. She knew there might be entries about her, but her emotions ping-ponged back and forth between hatred and bitterness toward Howard Hodges, to sympathy and anger at Hattie Mae for remaining quiet.

Although she understood the woman's fear, she would have died before she'd let the man hurt those girls.

For the first time in her life, the guilt she'd felt over the man's death abated slightly. She had murdered a man, yet if she hadn't, his reign of terror would have continued. No telling how many other girls might have suffered.

Her guilt over leaving Hattie Mae wavered—by killing Hodges, she had freed the woman of her worst nightmare and given her peace.

If she read farther, would she learn what had happened to the other girls when the center had closed?

DEKE PACED the wood-paneled den, hoping Elsie might come back downstairs and talk to him, but finally gave up and checked his computer. Brack had e-mailed him a message saying he was still trying to track down Elsie's father, then sent an attachment. Deke opened it up and scanned the information.

Elsie's father had accumulated three aliases while he'd traipsed Elsie around the States. He also had a rap sheet, which included charges of assault and battery, robbery and gambling.

Elsie, also, had been arrested. Twice, each time

under a pseudonym before her father dumped her, and three times after she'd left Wildcat Manor.

Damn. The juvenile records were sealed, but three arrests included charges of trespassing on private property and public disorderly conduct. Her last arrest was for possession of a firearm, but it had been pleaded down by a court-appointed attorney, who claimed she had grabbed the gun from a street thug who had attacked her. She'd been living on the streets.

He dropped his head into his hands with a growl. He'd thought he'd had a tough life growing up without a father, but Elsie had had no one. She'd been vulnerable, defenseless, all alone in the world. Yet she'd turned out to be a beautiful, sensitive woman who wanted to help others now.

He had to help her.

A noise cut into his thoughts, and he heard thrashing around upstairs. Something hit the floor and crashed. Then a shrill scream pierced the air.

Deke grabbed his gun and took off running.

HE HAD HER NOW. His hands clutched her neck as he dragged her along. He would punish her for ruining his night. For trying to protect the little girls.

He was a monster.

He drugged them and made them do despicable things. And then he took the infants....

The shrill cry of the newborn tore at her insides,

and she ran toward the garden to hide. Bugs crawled up her skin as she buried herself in the thicket of brush. Leaves and twigs snapped beneath his feet as he searched for her. His loud growl pierced the air.

"I'm going to find you, and when I do, you'll be sorry." His boots crunched the frozen ground, ice cracking beneath his weight. She peered through the blades of dead greenery, trying to be invisible. She wanted to run and run and never come back.

But she couldn't. She had to stay here. Protect the younger ones.

He leaned closer, raking his hands through the weeds. He was close now, so close. She shrank back, burying herself so deeply, the weeds choked her. Her stomach heaved as the scent of his breath whirled through the frigid air near her face. Then his eyes pierced the tiny opening in the bushes.

Her heart stopped as she held her breath and waited.

But his hand snaked through the foliage and he wound his fingers around her arm. She screamed. She had to escape....

HE SHOOK HER, and she twisted frantically to escape him. "No!"

"Elsie!"

She jerked away and fought, kicking and screaming, but he pinned her arms above her head. She closed her eyes, trying to block out his presence. She knew what he would do to her now. Fighting would only make his punishment harsher. She had to lie perfectly still, shut him out....

"Elsie, wake up, it's me, Deke." He cupped both her hands into one of his, then stroked a finger down her cheek. "Honey, wake up, it's me, Deke. You're safe now."

The husky voice, the whispered word of affection, battled its way through her senses, and she opened her eyes, heaving for air. Deke's chiseled face stared at her, his eyes dark and angry, but his gruff voice rumbled out allaying her nerves.

"You're safe now, Elsie. I'm here, just me. I've got you."

Not bothering to think, she threw herself into his arms, savoring the rise and fall of his chest as he held her. He rocked her back and forth for several minutes, murmuring reassuring nonsensical words as he pressed her face into his strong shoulder and stroked her back. She buried herself in his massive hold, allowing him to ease the tension from her body. The scent of his masculinity slid over her senses. Deke was fierce, hard and tough, the most masculine man she'd ever met, yet he was so gentle that tears filled her eyes.

"Elsie, tell me about your nightmares," he whispered in a husky voice.

She shook her head, but he kissed her softly on the forehead. Then he pressed a kiss to her cheek, and wiped away her tears with the pad of his thumb.

"Please talk to me, Elsie. I promise I'll understand."

"He was after me," she said in a low voice.

"Who? Your father or Mr. Hodges?"

"Hodges."

"What was he going to do?"

"Punish me."

He swallowed, the coarse skin of his beard stubble brushing her skin. "For what?"

"Because I tried to protect the younger girls."

"So he took his rage out on you?"

She nodded against him, then angled her face sideways to hide the shame. He lowered himself down beside her on the bed, and cradled her in his arms, spooning her with his warmth as he rubbed her cold arms with his hands. She felt the hard planes of his chest against her back, felt the heat of his sex as it stirred into her hip, and for a moment, fear tightened her belly.

"Relax, and go back to sleep," he said in a gruff voice. "I promise not to hurt you, Elsie."

Fresh tears welled in her eyes. No, she didn't think he would physically. But what if she fell for him? What if she…actually cared for him? Would he walk away one day as everyone else in her life had, and leave her alone?

She couldn't bear to put her heart on the line and have it broken.

Still, she inhaled his scent, sank into his embrace, for the first time in her life, accepting solace from a man. Just for tonight, she'd let him hold her. But tomorrow, when dawn brightened the gray sky and the night shadows drifted into daytime horrors that she could manage on her own, she'd stand alone again.

The way she'd always done. The way she always would.

THE NEXT MORNING, Deke rose before dawn, his efforts at rest a failure. How could he sleep with Elsie lying next to him, her butt cradled against his thighs, the soft feminine scent of her wafting toward him with each breath she took?

Summoning every ounce of strength he possessed, he dragged himself away from the temptation to wake her and fulfill the fantasies he'd entertained during the long night.

A fresh layer of snow had fallen, creating crystal patterns on the window, and ice-laden tree branches scraped the glass. The rumble of the ancient furnace barely cut into the chill. He built a fire in the room to keep Elsie warm, and left her sleeping.

After spending a night next to her, holding her in his arms, his sex throbbed, the continual erection he'd felt all night aching relentlessly. He had to go for a run in the woods. Clear his head. Regain control.

Give Elsie time to rest, to realize that they'd spent the night together, had shared a bed, and he had kept his promise. He wouldn't do anything she didn't want.

He strode downstairs, yanked on a denim shirt and his bomber jacket, then stepped onto the porch, scanning the area to make sure it was safe before he fled into the forest to check on the falcons.

The morning air and scents of wildlife invigorated Deke, although images of Elsie filled his head, too. He searched a five-mile perimeter, looking for injured birds or other animals that needed help, but thankfully found nothing. On his way back, he paused to study the sounds—trees crunching beneath his boots, the swirl of the kestrel's wingspan as it soared above him, the chatter of squirrels and chipmunks scouring for food. As he neared the edge of the forest near Wildcat Manor, he spotted a pickup truck in the drive, and he headed toward it, wondering who had ventured out this early and why they had come to the orphanage.

Fear knotting his stomach, he crossed his arms

and squared his shoulders as a salt-and-pepper-haired, barrel-chested man wearing jeans and a flannel shirt slid from the seat.

"Morning. I'm Jeb Waddell. The lady that lives here asked me to come out and do some repairs."

"Deke Falcon." He extended his hand in offering and the man shook it.

"Don't really know why she's bothering with this old house. I heard it's haunted."

Deke frowned. "She has her reasons."

Jeb removed his cap and scratched at his near-bald head. "I told her I'd do what I could, but if I hear anything funny like ghosts and stuff, I'm out of here."

Deke chuckled. So the burly man was afraid of ghosts.

"Where should I start?"

"Why don't you clean up the grounds outside first. After breakfast Elsie can tell you what she wants you to do next."

Jeb nodded, circled to the back of his truck and removed a wheelbarrow. He pushed it to the side of the house, then pulled on work gloves and began hacking at some of the weeds.

Deke went inside and brewed a pot of coffee, then logged on to his computer to see what else he could dig up on the town. A few minutes later, Elsie emerged, dressed in jeans and a loose-fitting blue sweater. His body instantly reacted, but he tamped down his desire when he saw the wary look on her face.

"I'm sorry about last night," Elsie said as she poured herself a cup of coffee.

"Why?" he asked in a low voice. "Because of the nightmare or because you let me hold you?"

She averted her eyes, a blush staining her cheeks. "Both."

He went to her, then stroked her hand gently. "I'm not sorry you let me hold you, Elsie. It felt good. Right."

Her gaze shot to his. "Deke—"

"Shh." He pressed a finger to her lips to ward off her argument. "The guy you hired is outside pulling weeds. I want to go to town and talk to Dr. Mires and Burt Thompson this morning."

She nodded. "I was going to do that myself."

"We'll go together."

"Deke—"

"You're not going anywhere without me. It's too dangerous."

She opened her mouth to protest, but a shout erupted from the back. He rushed to the French doors and saw Jeb running toward the house. Deke threw open the door. "What's wrong?"

"I...I went around to the garden area, thought I'd clean it up first."

"And?" Deke pressed.

"Some animals were sniffing and digging around, so I leaned over to see what they were doing." He gulped, eyes wide, sweat pouring down his face. "There's a...a body buried back there."

Elsie gasped in horror, her legs folding beneath her. Deke grabbed her for support.

"I'll go check it out, Elsie."

Elsie had to go, too. Had to see who the body belonged to.

What if it was her baby? No, her little girl was buried in the woods beneath that oak tree by the pond. Miss Hattie Mae had shown her the grave so she could visit and have closure.

She inhaled sharply. "I'll go with you."

Deke gave her an odd look, then hurried out the back door following the older man. Her nightmare from the evening before rose to haunt her. It had been so vivid. The weeds choked the life from the garden, the stench of death and decay—it was just as she remembered as a kid when she'd hidden in the thicket.

"It's back here," Jeb said. "I like gardening, so I was checking out this one to see how much work I'd have to do to revive it."

Deke stopped at a small clearing, then Jeb pointed to the right where a bobcat clawed at the ground. At the sound of their approach, the animal lifted its head, growled, then looked up at Elsie and

Deke with teeth bared. A small bone protruded from its mouth, and Elsie's stomach clenched.

Deke gestured for her to wait, while he inched closer, speaking softly, his voice tranquil, hypnotic. She held her breath, praying the bobcat didn't attack him, while Jeb backed away.

Deke grew very calm, then stooped to the bobcat's eye level and continued talking, but Elsie couldn't discern the words. The animal paused from his digging, and seemed entranced by Deke's voice. It was almost as if Deke shared a secret language with the wild creature. Finally, he moved close enough to stroke the animal's head, slowly, gently, just as he'd touched her. In seconds, he'd formed a connection with the animal that went beyond reason. That part of him that exuded raw masculinity mirrored the animal's. But their inner souls must be connected, similar.

Time stood still for a brief second, then finally the bobcat turned and trotted off.

"Lord, almighty," Jeb muttered "I ain't never seen anything like that, mister."

Deke shrugged, then approached the grave with a solemn expression. Elsie wanted to look, to make certain they hadn't uncovered her baby's grave, but fear held her in its clutches.

"It's human, isn't it?" Jeb asked.

"Yes," Deke said in a strained voice. "It looks like the body belonged to a little girl."

"A girl?" Elsie asked in a shaky voice.

Deke nodded. "Looks like she was about eleven years old. She's been here for a long time."

Elsie's throat closed. Thank God it wasn't her baby. But if it was a child's body, then it was probably one of the girls who'd lived at the orphanage. Hodges had threatened the girls that if they tried to leave, he'd punish them severely. Over the years, a few girls had disappeared, but he and Hattie Mae claimed that they had found homes for them. She'd thought the girls lucky.

But what if he had killed them instead? Would they find more bodies buried if they searched for them?

Chapter Eleven

Deke didn't trust the sheriff but he had to call him. A half hour later, he appeared with his deputy, along with a crime scene unit from the county and the local medical examiner, Jim Franks. They studied the grave, removed the body of the young girl, then the sheriff questioned Jeb while the CSI team examined the area for evidence. Elsie had retreated inside to read more of the journal, the tension between her and the sheriff palpable.

Sheriff Bush paced around the gravesite, his brows furrowed. "It looks like she's been here around ten or eleven years."

"Can you tell the cause of death?" Deke asked.

"I won't know until I examine the bones."

Deke folded his arms across his chest and studied the medical examiner. "You've lived in Wildcat for years. Did you ever get called to the orphanage?"

Franks's face twitched, as if the question made him uneasy, then shook his head. "I only make calls when someone dies."

"You didn't know about this girl?"

Frank's face flamed red with anger. "Of course not."

Deke narrowed his eyes. "Did you perform an autopsy on Hodges?"

The sheriff and Franks exchanged an uncomfortable look. "Didn't see any reason to," Franks said. "Fire killed him."

Deke frowned. If they had suspected that Elsie or someone else had started the fire, they would have performed an autopsy for evidence. Odd.

"What about the infants who were born here?" Deke asked.

Franks stood, using his palms to smooth down his dress pants. "For a stranger in town, you sure do ask a lot of questions."

"I'm a friend of Elsie Timmons's," he said, wanting them to know he was watching her back. "I have reason to believe Hodges abused the girls here. Since this girl is dead, I'm wondering if he killed her. And if he did, he might have hurt others."

"We never got any reports of violence out here," Bush said.

Deke hissed. How blind could they have been? "How about problems in childbirth? Did you ever lose any of the infants or any of the girls during delivery?"

Elsie reappeared at the edge of the woods, her heart pounding while she waited on the medical examiner's reply.

Would he tell them about her baby? Had he come out to the manor the night her child was born? Had they performed an autopsy?

She didn't think so. They'd certainly never mentioned it. And she had been too young and traumatized to ask the right questions. They had informed her that her baby died, then whisked it away in the night to bury it. She hadn't even gotten to see her little girl or hold her and tell her goodbye.

"No," Franks said. "Doc Mires took good care of the girls. I don't recall any problems with any deliveries or any of the teenagers." He glanced down at the skeletal remains of the young girl, then back up at Deke. "Mires and Thompson arranged for nice families to raise the babies. It worked out well for the unwed mothers and the parents who couldn't have children."

Elsie swallowed back the bitter, painful memories.

Deke placed a steadying hand to her back as she approached. "Elsie?"

She couldn't look him in the eye. If she'd only known the extent of Hodges's abuse, she would have run away and told on him. But her silence had cost girls their lives.

"Mr. Hodges did abuse the girls," she said as she faced the sheriff. "I didn't think he killed anyone, but he used to punish us with violence and deprivation. Sometimes he locked us in the dark closet, sometimes he took us to the basement and…beat us. And then…" Her voice broke.

"Then what, Miss Timmons?" the sheriff asked in a hard tone.

"He molested a few of the girls, got them pregnant, then forced them to give up their babies." She inhaled, trying to calm her roaring heart.

"If that's true, why didn't you report it? Tell someone?" Sheriff Bush asked.

Elsie's spine stiffened at his tone. He didn't believe her. "Because we were too afraid. I…was too afraid. If we ever talked or tried to escape, he made us suffer."

Bush scowled. "It's hard to believe someone didn't report it."

"Maybe they tried to, and no one listened," Deke said. "From what I've heard and seen in this town, the people turned a blind eye to the kids in need."

"I don't like what you're insinuating," Bush said.

"And I don't like the way this town has tried to cover up things," Deke barked. "For God's sake, you were the sheriff and you let this travesty go on."

Elsie cleared her throat. "I...there are more bodies."

The sheriff pivoted abruptly, the medical examiner cocked his head in question, and Deke closed the distance to her. "What? Did you find another one, Elsie?"

"No." Her voice wavered. "While you were out here, I went inside and read more of Hattie Mae's journal. In it, she mentioned two more girls' deaths. Hodges hid their bodies behind the walls in the basement."

DR. MIRES SKIMMED his old files, memorizing as many of the dates and names as he could. He had to shred the material. That Falcon man and Elsie Timmons were bound to show up at his office sooner or later, and he wanted to be able to honestly tell them that his files had been destroyed. They need not know that he had just done so himself.

Granted most of the adoptions were technically legal, and many infants had been placed in loving homes with the unwed mothers' consent, but there were a couple of questionable cases....

If word got out that he had covered up for Hodges's indiscretions, his reputation would be ruined.

He skimmed another file, then ran it through the shredder. Better that the files disappeared. In fact, he should have done it years ago to avoid a paper trail. He'd promised the parents of the adoptees total anonymity and he owed them. The adopted children didn't need their lives uprooted, either. He'd seen news stories where children and families were torn apart, and he wouldn't wish that pain on anyone. Some of the people were even his friends, family, the children safe and happy right here in Wildcat.

No, Elsie Timmons couldn't destroy their lives. He wouldn't allow it.

A knock sounded at the door, and he pushed his wire-rims up his nose, sweat beading on his upper lip. Donna, Thompson's secretary, stepped inside with a worried look on her face. Beside her stood Eleanor Cross, his sister. Heaven alive, had the two women paired up in panic?

He heaved a deep breath. "Ladies, what can I do for you today?"

Donna closed the door, a terrified look in her eyes. "You can assure us that our children are safe. That you've kept silent."

"I'm shredding the files now," he said, his nerves zinging. "Soon, any reference to the adoptions will be erased completely."

Eleanor suddenly withdrew a small pistol and aimed it at him. His eyes widened. Surely she hadn't gone mad. "Eleanor, now calm down, honey. I told you I'm taking care of it."

"What if they make you tell them?" she asked in a high-pitched voice.

"Don't be ridiculous," he snapped, although he instantly regretted his comment when she released the safety on the gun.

"I know you've had attacks of conscience over the years," Donna said with a frown. "That you regretted getting involved with Hodges."

"I did regret some things," he admitted. "I never wanted the girls to be harmed. And when I found out that he was hurting them…" He dropped his head forward, the memory of the day he'd caught Hodges seared into his brain. "I tried to stop him. God knows I tried."

"But you were in too deep by then, weren't you?" Donna asked.

Hell, yes. His own wife had wanted a baby so badly. All the miscarriages. The fertility treatments. The disappointments. At last he'd seen his chance for a child. And then Eleanor…

After that, helping the girls had come naturally. He was a doctor. He wanted to treat them in return for the gift he'd been given. But then the lies trapped him. If he'd quit the orphanage, Hodges would have ruined him. And if he hadn't worked with him, Hodges would have found someone else, someone not as qualified, someone who might not have cared about the girls' health care or the infants. Then what would have happened to them?

It had been a no-win situation. When Elsie Timmons had started that fire…

She had been a godsend that had ended it all.

Yet now she was back again. Guilt weighed on him. He should tell her the truth.

But he didn't have the courage.

"I see the wheels turning in your head now," Eleanor said. "I know you'll crack if they push you."

He denied her accusation, although he'd never had a good poker face. He was old and tired and the lies had eaten away at his soul. He laid the folder down, stared at it and wanted to do the right thing. But the right thing for one person would hurt another.

Eleanor slowly walked toward him, her hand shaking. "Shred it," she ordered.

He didn't move. He simply stared at her, some part of his inner being snapping from the guilt. "Put the gun down, sis. If you kill me, you'll go to prison and then you'll lose your children forever."

Eleanor lifted the weapon higher, and he braced himself for death. Then his son's face flashed into his mind, and he wavered. He wanted to see his boy graduate one day. And he couldn't bear the thought of him being disappointed in his father. If the truth was revealed, he would be. He might even go looking for his birth mother and that would devastate the boy's mother.

Desperate, he reached for the weapon. He'd come too far to give up now. "Let it go, Eleanor. I'll take care of things like I always have."

But Eleanor's hand wobbled, and he heard the click of the gun's chamber....

AN EERIE CHILL SLID UP Elsie's spine as she entered the dark basement. Pungent, rancid odors swirled around her, even more acrid than they had been when she was a child. Dark shadows claimed the corners, rising and drifting through the dank concrete-floored room like monsters. From the right side, the shrill scream of a baby's cry shattered the silence, the hollow wail of a young girl in pain following.

The sound was her own voice. Her own baby's cry. Its futile struggle for a breath. The moment the baby grew quiet.

Or the screams of the girls who lay behind the walls?

She shuddered, remembering the cold, hard clink of medical tools on steel tables, the plea for help from the room on the left where the doctor sometimes examined the girls. The smaller room in the back where Hodges took them for his own sick pleasure.

A loud noise crashed into her reverie, and she

blinked and saw Deke pounding a hatchet into the stone. The sheriff and his deputy worked in a different area, all diligently searching to see if the girls' bodies truly lay behind the walls.

She hugged her arms around herself, trying desperately to hold herself together, but her legs felt like jelly, and dizziness made the room spin. A blinding sea of light and darkness trapped her in the past. She should help, do something. She should have done more back then.

The seconds ticked by as if she'd fallen into a vortex and couldn't escape. Tick. Tock. Tick. Tock. Would the cries of the children ever stop?

"I found something." Deke lowered his tool, and swiped at his forehead, perspiration dampening his hair and trickling down his neck. She bit her lip and stood, then hesitated. She wasn't sure she could look.

"It's a body," the sheriff said in a flat tone.

"I found another one!" the deputy shouted.

"Oh, my God," Elsie whispered. "It's true."

Hadn't she been afraid for her life each time he approached her? She'd cowered like a terrified animal, and had obeyed him out of fear. Just like Hattie Mae.

The coroner had gone to the morgue with the first body, but the sheriff phoned him to return and collect the others.

Elsie's stomach lurched at the sight of a bone

protruding from the opening. She ran up the stairs, then into the bathroom and fell to her knees, purging the contents of her stomach. If Hodges had killed the girls because they disobeyed him, or because they refused to give up their children, he would have eventually killed her. And what if they found more bodies?

The guilt she'd felt over Hodges's death drained from her. She was glad he was dead. No longer would she pray for forgiveness. In fact, her only regret was that she should have killed him sooner.

DEKE'S MIND SPUN with the reality of the truths they'd uncovered. Girls murdered and buried on the property and inside the house. No wonder people thought ghosts lived in the manor, and believed the devil lived in the forest.

How had Elsie survived this horrendous place? And to do so, and have a heart of gold, to want to devote herself to helping others and turn this place around—it was a miracle.

No, she was a miracle. Her inner strength amazed him. He'd never admired a woman more.

He fisted his hands, knowing emotions were dangerous. He had to concentrate. Think like a detective.

The sheriff, his deputy and the crime scene unit finally finished, and Deke went upstairs in search of Elsie. She hadn't looked well when she'd run from the room. He understood the feeling. His skin crawled, the inhumanity of Hodges's actions too horrific to believe.

He found Elsie pale and trembling, huddled on the sofa beneath a blanket, Hattie Mae's journal clutched in her hands.

He knelt beside her and stroked his hands up and down her arms. God, he wished she hadn't had to witness the gruesome scene in the basement. "Are you okay, Elsie?"

Her tearstained eyes met his. "I should have realized," she whispered raggedly.

"Don't, Elsie," he said in a gruff voice. "You did everything you could. You were just a kid yourself. You'd been abandoned and abused. You must have been terrified of Hodges."

She lowered her eyelashes and he pressed his palm against her cheek.

"Hodges was a monster, a psychopath. He never should have been around children." Deke tried to control his anger. "I'm going to find that social worker who was in charge of overseeing the orphanage and find out the reason she didn't report him."

"I don't understand, either," Elsie said, a hollow look in her eyes.

He gestured toward the journal. "Did you learn anything else from the book?"

She clamped her teeth over her lower lip. "He killed them because they didn't want to give up their babies. They defied him and tried to run away."

Deke's throat closed. Elsie had defied him by running away, too. If he'd caught her, he would have murdered her, too.

His stomach rolled, and he slid a hand in her hair, grateful she'd survived. "I'm glad you left this place, Elsie. I...you had amazing courage."

While he had depended on his brother to take care of things and had rebelled in anger, Elsie had been completely alone.

"Elsie—"

"You don't understand, Deke. I wasn't strong, I was terrified of him. I let him intimidate me, make me do things I didn't want to do. Such ugly things...."

His throat tightened. "I wish I could change the past, but I can't. We can change the future though. Together."

"You're right," she said, lifting her chin. "But I need to talk to Burt Thompson. He...may know more about the murders."

The sheriff lumbered in and Deke frowned. He thought the man had already left.

"Miss Timmons, I need Hattie Mae's journal as evidence." He gestured toward the book she held. "Is that it?"

"Yes." Elsie tightened her grip on the diary. "Can I finish it first?"

He shook his head. "It's part of an official murder investigation. I have to take it now. Hattie Mae might have told us more about those girls. Maybe *she* killed them out of jealousy."

"No. Mr. Hodges was responsible," Elsie said, still clinging to the book.

The sheriff extended his hand, his expression stony. "I still need it. There might be more victims mentioned later on."

Deke understood Elsie's reluctance to hand over the diary. She didn't trust the sheriff. And neither did he.

What if Bush destroyed the journal without revealing the contents?

IN SPITE OF THE COLD, sweat streamed down Sheriff Bush's face as he laid the journal on the seat beside him and headed into town. Thank God the Timmons girl had confessed that she'd found the book. He had to read its contents and see what Hattie Mae had said about Wildcat Manor, about who all had been involved. Him. Thompson. Mires.

How much did she actually know about the adoptions?

The sight of those teenagers' skeletons sent a sick feeling to his stomach that rippled all the way up into his throat. He had done a lot of good in this town over the years. But would it make up for the bad?

Would anyone understand the reason he'd turned his back against the goings-on at the orphanage?

Probably not. He was the sheriff, sworn to serve and protect. But choices weren't always divvied up into nice neat packages with easy answers. It was the hard ones that made you stretch your morals, made you cross the line.

He gripped the steering wheel as he rounded the mountain, gears grinding to keep the car from sliding on the ice, and barreling down the ridge. Although he already felt as if he was standing on the precipice, about to go over the edge.

He punched in Doc Mires's number. He had to ask him about the dead girls, tell him about the journal. Then he'd talk to Burton, find out why Elsie was still in town.

The phone rang several times, then clicked over to the answering service. Damn. He left a message for Mires to call him immediately, then phoned Thompson.

Thompson hissed as Bush explained about finding the bodies.

"Jesus, I had no idea he'd buried anyone out there."

"Me, neither," Bush said. "But do you honestly think anyone will believe us?"

"No," Thompson said in a shaky voice. "Not

when we covered up the adoption ring and Hodges's indiscretions."

"I wish to hell I'd never met Howard Hodges," Bush said. "I...didn't realize how sick the man was."

"Ditto."

A dull pain hit Bush's chest. He loosened his collar and tried to breathe. "I'll read Hattie Mae's journal. See what she revealed."

"I'll take care of the girl myself," Thompson said matter-of-factly.

Bush finally drew a breath. Thompson had always been the power behind the bunch. A money-hungry lawyer who never wavered from his own personal goals. The one without a conscience.

Bush hung up, then steered the car toward Donna's. He'd check on her and Eleanor, make sure they hadn't done something stupid. The last thing he needed was for them to panic, draw suspicion and make more trouble.

ELSIE CLUTCHED the sheer curtain and stared outside at the woods. Night had fallen over Wildcat Manor, the dismal grays and blacks surrounding the house a reminder of the bodies that had been found and removed today. What if there were others? More girls buried on the grounds?

Deke had ordered Elsie to lock the door with the gun by her side, while he hiked into the woods to check for anything suspicious. Grounds disturbed. Mounds that looked as if they might have served as a grave.

Elsie's palms grew sweaty, her heart pounding with fear. What if he found her baby's grave? Then he would know the truth….

Had Hattie mentioned Elsie's delivery in her journal? A few moments ago, Deke had called her courageous.

He would think differently if he learned that she'd been so starved for love and attention that she'd slept with a fifteen-year-old boy. That she'd been so stupid she'd gotten pregnant.

That she'd wanted the baby, but that she had failed her daughter.

Heart breaking, she could stand it no longer. She'd been away from her baby for ten years. Had run but had never escaped the guilt of leaving her behind.

Emotions raged inside her like the storms outside, and she grabbed her coat and the gun, then the flowers on the table that she'd purchased the day she'd bought the paint and fabric in town. Ten years and she'd never gotten to visit her baby's grave, never mourned by her side or brought flowers to her grave on her birthday or holidays.

She had to do it now.

Tugging her hood over her head, she fought the wind as she raced outside. Tears fell like raindrops onto the ground, her shoes clutching at the ice and mud to keep from falling. She dashed past the pond, hearing the shrill cry of death, then fled to the mound of trees at the edge of the forest near the garden until she located the tiny smattering of rocks that marked her baby's grave. Her hands trembled as she knelt, sorrow overwhelming her. Weeds and twigs covered the small area, and a feather from a hawk lay at the foot of the grave. It wasn't right that her baby didn't have a proper burial, that she had no marker, no tombstone to announce her birth, no epitaph to lay claim to her existence.

Elsie would rectify that matter.

Suddenly, that gesture, that recognition, meant more to her than her own shame.

The wind hurled debris across the mound, and she wiped it off angrily. The scent of whiskey floated toward her. Blood. Evil.

Someone was nearby.

She angled her head to look, but someone struck her from behind. Pain exploded in her temple. She gripped her head and tried to scream, but her voice died in the wind. Then her attacker shoved her facedown into the ground.

Chapter Twelve

Elsie gasped for air, eating dirt as she struggled to free herself from her attacker. She kicked backward, tried to jab her elbow into his stomach or groin, but missed. He yanked her head up, then slammed it against the hard ground again. Stars swam before her eyes, and she frantically reached for the gun. It was only inches away.

But just as her fingers connected with metal, he grabbed the weapon and pressed the barrel to the back of her head.

Fear rippled through her, just as regrets slammed into her conscience. Regrets for everything that had happened at Wildcat Manor. Regrets for not having the courage to face her mother.

But the wind fluttered the hawk's feather, and she focused on where it lay at the foot of her baby's grave. Deke's face flashed into her mind. The long chiseled nose. The broad jaw. His dark, enigmatic eyes. Regrets of a different kind poured through her.

She had never had a man kiss her as he had, never wanted a man so badly. But she hadn't had the courage to face him with the truth, either.

The man dug his knee into her back, and she winced, summoning her determination. She hadn't come this far to lie down and die.

No, she was a fighter.

Think about the streets. Hit the major points. Eyes, solar plexus, groin...

"You should have left town," he growled in her ear.

Elsie cried out in pain as he twisted one arm behind her back and stretched it upward at an odd angle. He was going to yank it from the socket.

"Now it's your turn to die, Elsie. " His foul breath brushed her cheek. "Would you like to go in the ground or in the basement walls like the others?"

Horror made her skin crawl. She punched backward with her elbow, straight into his groin. He howled and released the pressure on her arm. "Damn it, you bitch!"

She bucked backward, throwing him off balance, then rolled to her stomach and kicked both feet upward, connecting with his face. The gun toppled from his hands, and she scrambled to retrieve it.

"I think the basement—you always liked it down there, didn't you!" he bellowed.

She tried to lurch to her feet, but he yanked her foot to hold her back. Her hands dug into the ground for control, but he crawled after her, his face shrouded by the trees and a black cape. She kicked backward at his face with her other foot, then grabbed the gun. A second later, she rolled over, and reached for the trigger. The gunshot blasted the air, along with his growl of anger.

But she missed, and he lunged toward her.

THE BLOOD RUSHED to Deke's head.

The gunshot. Elsie was in trouble.

He took off running, his heart racing as he cut through the thick brush and trees, slinging mud from his boots as he went. The snap of twigs breaking and ice cracking splintered the air, mimicking his heavy breathing. Elsie had to be all right. She had to be.

He couldn't face finding her hurt or…no, he wouldn't think negative thoughts. Elsie was a fighter. Hopefully, *she* had fired the gun to save herself or get his attention. Or maybe someone else had fired it at her.

He never should have left her alone.

Above him, the hawks sailed, their long wing-spans crackling the air as they soared above the trees. Their flight pattern was taking him toward the manor, as if instinctively they sensed someone he cared about was in danger.

Seconds later, he burst through the clearing. "Elsie!"

He screamed her name repeatedly, scanning the edges of the forest, then followed the birds around the back of the house. "Elsie!"

Suddenly, he saw her on the ground, the gun aimed at a dark hooded figure. Fury ran through him, and he removed his .38, paused and aimed at the man's back. He pivoted slightly, and Deke took aim again, then pulled the trigger and sent a bullet flying. Elsie's attacker dodged sideways, and the bullet hit the tree beside him. Then he fled into the forest.

Deke's heart hammered in his chest as he raced through the edge of the woods to Elsie.

She pushed to her feet, turned and aimed her gun toward the woods and fired, but the man had disappeared.

"I didn't get him," she said, her eyes wild with terror and frustration.

He jerked her to him, and dragged her into his arms, shaking all over. "God, Elsie, are you all right?"

She slid the gun down to her side, and nodded against his chest. "My head hurts, but I'm fine. I wish I'd wounded him so we could find out who he is."

Deke examined her head. A lump was forming, but she should be okay. Deke cupped his hands around her face and forced her to look at him. "What were you doing out here? I told you to stay inside with the doors locked."

A dozen emotions flickered in her eyes. Anger. Fear. Grief.

"I...had to come out for a moment."

"Why? Do you have some kind of death wish, Elsie?"

She stepped backward, away from him. "You're angry with me?"

"Angry?" he shouted. "Angry?" His head roared with emotions. "Hell, yes, I'm angry. If you'd stayed inside, he wouldn't have gotten that close to you."

"I refuse to cower inside," Elsie argued. "I won't let anyone have that much control over me."

"Control?" his voice rose another decibel. *He* was completely out of control. "This has nothing to do with control. It has to do with keeping you alive."

She started to speak, but clamped her mouth shut, her eyes narrowing. "I have to find out who's trying to kill me," she said quietly.

"And I want to see you live to go home to your mother."

She hesitated. "I...I...want that, too."

He averted his eyes, feeling naked and exposed. His emotions were so raw they had to be showing on his face. "I...do you know how I felt when I heard that gunshot, Elsie?" His hands shook as he reached for her and pulled her closer to him. "Do you have any idea?" He dropped his head forward, leaning it against her forehead. "I thought he had you, that you might be dead."

His voice cracked, and he couldn't go on. Elsie's breath bathed his hand as she leaned her face into his hand. "I'm sorry, Deke. But after finding those girls' bodies today, I...had to go outside. The basement, the house, it smelled like death. I...could see the skeletons...."

He hissed in response. "I'm sorry I shouted at you. But you scared the hell out of me."

Unable to stop himself, he slid his hands into her hair, tipped her chin sideways and pressed his mouth to hers. He had to taste her. To hold her. To feel her heart beating beneath his own.

To know that she was alive.

One minute the kiss was gentle, yet the next his primal instincts kicked in, and he deepened the kiss, delving inside her mouth with his tongue to taste her sweetness and innocence.

Yes, he knew that part of Elsie wasn't innocent. She'd obviously seen the worst of men and life. Yet a tender shyness overlaid her physical response, as if she had never been loved before by a man.

From what he knew of her past, she probably hadn't.

But he would teach her about love. About yearning, touching and pleasuring.

He stroked her back, the long slender column of

her spine, the subtle curves that lay beneath the coat until his body was on fire, and he feared he might burn from the flame. He ached to take off their coats, lay her down in the midst of the forest where nature would serve as their bed, a perfect backdrop to the nature of man, of loving, of utilizing every physical sense.

But slowly, he reeled in his hunger. Elsie had been attacked moments ago. Had nearly been killed. She didn't need a man pushing her for sex. Especially outside on the cold ground.

What kind of man was he? Her needs came first.

"Deke—"

"Shh. I'm sorry, I had to hold you." His voice sounded gruff and strained to his own ears. Damn it, he was falling, hard, for Elsie Timmons. The lost little girl he had come to retrieve and take home. The woman he had vowed to protect.

A woman with secrets and distrust attached to her name.

Why the hell was he such a sucker?

He stumbled backward, trying to make sense of it all. Deke was a loner. He belonged in the wild. He couldn't be Elsie's savior. And he couldn't make love to her without committing his heart and soul.

Because Elsie deserved to be loved completely.

His foot hit a rock, and he jerked his head around, then noticed the flowers lying on the stone-cold ground. "What is this?" he asked. "Did you find another girl's grave?"

Her face paled to a white even more milky looking than the snow. Then tears overflowed and trickled down her cheeks. Her stare fell on the tiny mound of dirt, and his gut clenched. "Whose grave is it?" he asked, although something deep inside his soul whispered that he already knew the answer.

Her chin trembled as she looked into his eyes. "My baby's," she said in a haunted voice. "Mr. Hodges buried my little girl out here, and she's all alone."

As soon as Elsie muttered the confession, it struck her what she'd said. All along she'd tried so hard to keep her secret, yet when Deke had kissed her just now, she'd forgotten the pain. His touch had been so comforting, so passionate that her body still tingled with the yearning he'd evoked. She'd sunk into his arms and had an otherworldly moment where she'd sensed she'd come home. That Deke was her safe haven from the storm, that the two of them belonged together, that she was falling for him, and that he reciprocated the feelings.

That he would understand.

The wind whipped her hair around her face, and she dragged her gaze upward to meet his eyes, uncertainty plucking at her nerve endings like a harp player who didn't know the chords. Would she see shame? Disappointment? Pity?

"Your baby is buried here?" he asked as if he needed clarification that he'd understood her.

She nodded, biting on her lip, the tension between them stretching into an eternity.

Anger glittered in his eyes as he met her gaze. "How old were you?" he asked.

Mortification stung her cheeks at his cold voice. "Fourteen."

"Who was the father, Elsie?" He started to reach for her, but fisted his hands by his sides, and the old familiar fear immobilized her. Disappointment and pain at his reaction followed.

"*Your* father? Did he get you pregnant, or was it Hodges?"

A chill rippled through her at the fury in his tone. "God, no, not them."

"Then who was he?"

Her chest constricted. He was angry at her father and Hodges, but he was wrong. And once she told him the truth, he'd be mad at her. He'd probably walk away.

A few moments earlier, she thought she'd found her soul mate. Now she realized what a fool she'd been. She might as well tell him the truth and let him leave before she became any more enamored with him.

"Elsie?" His voice echoed so harshly in the wind that it sounded as if it were a million miles away. He had already slipped into the distance, the chasm separating them oceans apart.

"Neither one," she admitted, her face flaming hot. "I...my father left me alone all the time when I was a kid. He'd be gone for days."

If anything, his mouth quirked even tighter.

"By the time I was twelve, I was alone for weeks at a time. I was starved for attention, for love," she said in a self-deprecating tone. "I know that sounds pathetic, but it's true." She hesitated and tucked her hair behind one ear. "I met a guy on the streets one night when I was thirteen. He...was nice to me, promised me he'd show me a good time. He even asked me to run away with him."

Deke heaved a labored breath that rattled in the night air.

"Anyway, I was so lonely, I believed him. I let him... we had sex."

"He didn't force you?" Deke ground out.

"Not physically," she said in a haunted whisper. "But he was playing a game to entice me. Later that night, I found out that he was priming me for bigger prospects."

"What do you mean?"

"To go on the streets with him." She couldn't

face him and admit the rest, so she turned away, looked down at her baby's grave and remembered the consequences of that night. Although their baby hadn't been conceived in true love, she would have loved her anyway.

"He wanted to turn you into a prostitute," Deke said between clenched teeth. "Didn't he, Elsie? He made you think you owed him, then he was going to pimp you out?"

She nodded, clenching her arms around her waist. "When I realized what he wanted, I ran away from him."

"You went back home?"

"Not for a couple of days. Oddly, my father came home in the meantime. When he found out what happened, he kept me locked up. Then… when I discovered I was pregnant, he brought me here and left me."

"Son of a bitch."

She turned to face him. "I was a bad girl, Deke. I shouldn't have been so stupid. Shouldn't have thought that some guy would love me."

Deke swallowed. "Your father told you that, and you believed him?"

She shrugged. "Why wouldn't I? Everyone I'd ever known had abandoned me. I had to be bad for everyone to leave."

Deke shook his head, and Elsie spun away. "I understand that you're angry, that you hate me now, Deke. But now you know the truth, the reasons I can't go back to see my mother. How would she feel if she knew I killed a man, that I was a teenage unwed mother, that I had a baby who hadn't survived, that I left my daughter here in the ground without a proper burial?"

The pain and grief that had dogged her forever rose in her throat, and she decided to give Deke the easy way out. "I'll stay in my room while you pack." Not bothering to wait for an answer, she ran toward the house, battling the bitter elements.

Now that Deke knew everything, he'd run from her just as she had been running from herself all these years.

A TANGLE OF EMOTIONS swirled inside Deke. Rage for all the people who'd made Elsie think she didn't deserve love, that she was a bad child because others were too selfish to care for her. Anger at Hodges for his abuse, at her father for isolating her so much that she'd sought comfort from a stranger on the street, bitterness that he'd deserted her and her child. And poor Deanna…it would kill her to know how her daughter had suffered.

But she'd never turn Elsie away.

He scanned the woods again, wondering if he should have gone after the man who'd attacked

Elsie. But at the time, he hadn't been able to tear himself from her.

And he couldn't now.

He had to figure out who he wanted to hurt. Sheriff Bush was definitely suspect, along with the doctor who'd treated the girls, and that lawyer in town. He'd probably arranged the adoptions. He'd beat the answers out of them if he had to.

Now you know the truth, the reasons I can't go back to see my mother.... I left my daughter here in the ground without a proper burial....

The agony in her voice had been so intense it had ripped at his gut.

Determined to prove to her that she was wrong, that he didn't think she was bad, that her mother wouldn't, either, he strode inside, kicking at the ice and dirt, venting his rage from his own childhood. His rage toward everyone who'd hurt her by promising to bring them all down. He wished Hodges was alive so he could kill him with his bare hands. And when Brack found Elsie's father...

God help him, he didn't know what he would do to the man.

The door screeched as he pushed it open. He walked into the kitchen, then the den, searching for Elsie, and found her by the fire, staring into it as if she was reliving the nightmare when Hodges had died. Or maybe she was thinking about her child.

He approached her slowly, his pulse pounding like a jackhammer.

"Elsie, I want you to listen," he said in a gruff tone.

Her quiet breath shook in the darkness. "I don't blame you. Just go, Deke."

He strode toward her, then turned her so she had to face him. "Listen to me. I'm not angry at you, I'm angry *for* you. In fact, I'm furious at all the people who hurt you in the past. That young boy who took advantage of you, your father for ripping you away from Deanna, then deserting you when you needed him most. And Hodges for all that he put you through." She dropped her chin forward and shook her head, but he forced her chin back up, made her look into his eyes.

"Don't you get it? I care about you. And I'm not walking away." Emotions reverberated in his voice, but he didn't hold back. He'd put his heart on the line if it would help her. "You were only a kid, Elsie. You looked for love wherever you could find it, just like any child would. You're not to blame."

"But—"

"No, buts. When my dad was arrested, I was mad, too. I rebelled and got into all kinds of trouble with the law. If it hadn't been for my brothers and my mother…I don't know what would have happened to me."

"But you're strong and they love you—"

"That's it, Elsie. I still acted out, got into trouble, and I had other people who loved me. You had no one."

She quivered beneath his touch, and he dragged her toward him. "Sweetheart, I'd do anything if I could go back and change the past for you, take away the pain."

"I was so lonely," Elsie admitted in a tearstained voice. "But I shouldn't have slept with that boy."

"He should have used protection. But he was a sick little bastard. *You* were innocent. He knew exactly what he was doing. That makes him the bad guy, Elsie."

She gripped his arms as if to steady herself. "I don't want my mother to know. I can't see the look on her face—"

"Deanna won't be angry or disappointed in you. She loves you and has waited too long to see you again to let anything interfere."

Knowing he had to make her believe him, he lowered his mouth and kissed her one more time. Her lips felt supple, sweet, tasted like fear and desire all twisted together, and he gentled the kiss, determined not to push her.

He had to prove to her that he cared, that he would stand beside her.

"We're going to find out who's trying to hurt you here," Deke said. "And when things are settled, once you go back and see your mother, we'll give your little girl a proper burial."

"With a monument and everything?" Elsie asked. "She deserves that, Deke. She needs to have her name carved in gold and a special Bible verse."

"Anything you want, Elsie." He kissed her again, this time deeper and more passionate. "Anything at all."

HE STARED AT Doc Mires's dead body, a mixture of regret and relief flowing through his veins.

It was better this way. The old coot would probably have given in and talked sooner or later. Mires was such a damn sap, he was surprised he hadn't already spilled his guts.

And then where would *he* be?

His instincts kicking in, he removed the key to the doctor's medicine cabinet, then hurried and unlocked it, removing the supplies he needed. For the first time ever, he wondered if he would be able to survive without the doctor. Over the years, Mires had continued to treat him. Had done so in private, offering him painkillers when he needed them.

What would he do now if his stash ran low?

He stuffed his pockets full, then closed the cabinet door, wiped off the key and placed it back in Mires's pocket. No one would know he'd stolen the drugs.

Hell, no one would know he had even been

here. He was a ghost in this town, the devil some called him.

A chuckle rumbled from his belly.

It was true. And he'd haunt the people here forever.

Chapter Thirteen

Elsie almost believed that Deke really cared for her. Yet a part of her still held out. Her uncertainties and fears had kept her prisoner for years. Unchaining herself from the guilt and feelings of betrayal would take more time.

But his words chipped away at her bindings slightly.

"Elsie?" Deke traced a finger along her jaw, slowly, tenderly

"Yes?"

"I want to go into town and question Dr. Mires."

"Why?"

"He lied and said that he never lost any babies here. But you lost your child."

A wave of pain engulfed Elsie. "He lied about the abuse, too. I know he treated a few of the girls for injuries."

Again, that spark of anger flared in Deke's eyes,

but this time she understood it was targeted toward Hodges and Mires, not her.

"He might even know the identities of the girls buried here."

Elsie nodded. "Why do you think he protected Hodges?" Elsie slid her hand along Deke's arm, savoring the warmth of his body. "I don't remember him being cruel. In fact, he was always nice to the girls. And he seemed sincere about giving us prenatal care, and delivering healthy infants."

Deke shrugged. "Maybe he got kickbacks on the adoptions. Hodges was probably selling the babies."

A sick knot clenched in Elsie's stomach. But Deke's theory made sense.

"Feel up to paying him a visit?" Deke asked.

Elsie nodded. "Yes, it's time I face him."

Deke took her hand, and they hurried to his car. The warmth of the cab enveloped them as Deke drove down the mountain. The ironclad grip he had on the steering wheel mirrored the mask of control he kept on his emotions. But she'd glimpsed more of him the past few days, a deep raw need that had spiked her own.

She wanted this man. And she was going to let him make love to her. Eventually. The thought of touching him so intimately stirred her senses and sent mind-numbing sensations to her belly. As if he sensed the change in her, he covered her hand with one of his, the silent implication that he didn't intend to leave her side, hacking away at the defensive wall she'd built around herself.

A few minutes later, he parked in front of Dr. Mires's office.

"Are you sure you're up to this?"

"Absolutely." She squeezed his hand. "The sooner we get answers, the sooner I can open the teen center."

He climbed out and walked around to the passenger side, but she met him in front of the Range Rover. Together they entered the doctor's office, the feel of his hand on her back comforting.

Deke muttered a curse. "It looks like we're too late. Someone beat us here."

Elsie gasped. Dr. Mires was slumped over his desk, pale and still. Blood seeped from his chest onto his desk and papers.

He had been murdered.

"His medical files are ruined," Deke said with another curse as he gestured to the shredded papers on the floor.

Elsie staggered slightly and started to touch the desk, but Deke cut her off. "Don't touch anything, Elsie."

She dropped her hand immediately. He was right. She didn't want her fingerprints anywhere. If the sheriff found out about her baby, he might accuse her of killing Mires out of some twisted need for revenge.

Deke growled. "All the files connected with Wildcat Manor have been destroyed."

Hope for finding out anything on the girls died.

Elsie cleared her throat. "Who do you think shredded them—Dr. Mires or his killer?"

DEKE PHONED THE SHERIFF. As much as he hated working with Bush, he had to report a crime or the ignorant man might try to pin it on him and Elsie.

"Sheriff, I'm at Dr. Mires office. You'd better get over here ASAP. Mires has been murdered."

A string of expletives exploded over the line. "I'll be right there. Don't touch anything," Bush ordered.

"We haven't."

"We?"

"Miss Timmons is with me."

"That figures," Bush bellowed. "That girl has done nothing but cause trouble ever since she arrived in town. Just like those orphan teens did years ago."

"Elsie had nothing to do with this," Deke barked. "She happens to be the victim here. And if you were any kind of sheriff, you'd be on top of the threats against her, just like you should have been on top of the abuse taking place years ago."

Rage pumped through his system as Deke ended the call. For Elsie's sake, he gathered his self-control. If he didn't, he'd get locked up for assaulting Bush when he arrived.

Five minutes later, the sheriff roared up, siren blasting. No sooner had he stepped inside than the medical examiner appeared, along with another crime scene unit from the county. The sheriff cordoned off the area while the group immediately went to work, assessing the body and collecting evidence.

"We'll need both your footprints and fingerprints," one of the CSI team members said.

Elsie hesitated, and Deke realized she was thinking of her police record. But they had discovered the body and had no choice but to cooperate.

"What were you two doing here?" Bush asked.

"We came to question Dr. Mires about the dead bodies we found earlier."

"I've known Mires a long time," Bush said. "He had nothing to do with those deaths. And he'd never cover up a murder."

Deke made a disgusted sound. "How about you, Sheriff?" He leaned so close to Bush's face that Bush flinched.

"I don't like your implications, boy."

"And I don't like the fact that you warned Miss Timmons and me to leave town when we arrived." He folded his arms across his chest. "With multiple murders now, it's time to call in the FBI. I have a feeling they'll be very interested in learning about the adoptions, the abuse and the murders at Wildcat Manor."

"Get this straight, Falcon. I didn't cover up those murders. And we don't need the Feds. I can handle this case."

Deke speared him with a lethal look. "Like you took care of those orphans?"

Bush twitched. "I didn't know Hodges was abusing them or I would have stopped it!"

"You're lying," Deke said.

"Get out of here before I lock you up for interfering with an investigation."

Elsie tugged at Deke's sleeve. "Let's go, Deke. He's not going to help us any more than he did years ago."

Sheriff Bush jabbed a finger at Deke. "I told you I knew nothing of the abuse and that's the truth."

"And the adoptions?" Deke asked.

"I said get of here," Sheriff Bush ordered.

Deke's instincts kicked in. He would call the Feds, but he wanted even more to tell them. "That's the real reason you don't want us around, isn't it?" Deke lowered his tone to a menacing pitch. "You're afraid we'll find information on the adoptions. Did you adopt one of the babies yourself?"

DID YOU ADOPT one of the babies yourself?

Deke Falcon's questions hit far too close to home for Sheriff Bush to draw a moment of peace.

He harbored no false illusions that Falcon would give up his quest. Or that he wouldn't call the Feds. And Elsie Timmons was nothing like the frightened obedient girl who'd first come to Wildcat Manor, seeking approval, love and a place to hide.

She had set the fire that had killed Hodges. But he hadn't pressed charges, hadn't looked for her, because frankly, he did have a conscience, and he was glad she'd escaped.

But he'd never imagined that she'd return. As far as he was concerned, the adoptions had all been legal. The babies were better off. The teens had been given a chance for a new life without a kid in tow. And young couples had been handed a gift.

What was the harm?

Except for Hodges—he had gone too far. Some of the infants had been his….

The ill feeling he'd had when he'd first discovered the truth still plucked at his humanity.

Damn it, it was too late now. He couldn't let the lives of those parents and their adopted children be ruined because of Elsie Timmons and some damned obsessive P.I. What was done was done.

He glanced at Mires, sorry he was dead and wondering who had shot him. Sweat beaded on his forehead as he contemplated the possibilities. He had to know for sure.

The M.E. looked up at him with a sour, worried expression. "Estimated cause of death, gunshot to the heart. He bled out."

"What type of gun?"

"Looks like a .38."

Sheriff Bush gave a brisk nod. Did Donna or Eleanor have a .38?

The CSI team was wrapping up. "We have several sets of prints," Aaron, one of the regulars he'd dealt with before, reported. "We'll let you know what we find."

"Thanks. I'll be waiting on your report." He scrubbed a chunky fist over his chin. "Do you have anything on those vics we found at Wildcat Manor?"

Aaron's face grew solemn. "Not yet. But we're getting dental records from Dr. Simmerman. We should have IDs soon."

"Then we can run them and let the parents know." That is, if they could find them. It had been ten years. Some of the kids had been runaways while some had been unwanted, their parents having abandoned them. But he had a job to do and he would do it.

He also had to cover his ass.

He jotted down notes about the crime scene, position of the body, items on Mires's desk, the shredded files and decided to take a look through

Mires's computer. But when he went to access the files, he discovered the computer had crashed.

Had the killer destroyed the files and crashed the doctor's computer to get rid of the evidence linking them to the orphanage, or had Mires?

When the CSI team finished and Franks had completed his initial report, they loaded Mires onto the stretcher to transport him for an autopsy. Sheriff Bush had to find Donna and Eleanor. He had a lot of questions for both of them.

He only prayed they hadn't killed Mires. If so, he had to find a way to cover for them. It was the only way to keep Donna in his life.

ELSIE WAS STILL FUMING from the sheriff's hostile reaction. But Deke assured her that Bush's attitude had more to do with being frightened because they were close to finding the truth than it did with his integrity or desire to find justice.

Could Deke be right? Although when Deke had asked Bush if he'd adopted one of the children, he'd reacted suspiciously. Then Bush denied having a child, which was easily verifiable. But that didn't mean he didn't know someone who had adopted a baby from the manor. Someone he cared about and wanted to protect.

For that, she couldn't blame him. She sympathized with both birth mothers and parents who adopted. If her child was alive and had been adopted out, what would she do now? Look for her? Let her little girl stay in the secure family who had taken her in at birth, or uproot her world?

It was a moral dilemma that she didn't have to face, but others would if the entire truth were revealed.

Five minutes later, they pulled up to the medical examiner's office just as he arrived. The ambulance delivered Mires's body, while she and Deke cut Franks off at the entrance.

"If you continue to follow me, I'm going to file a restraining order and charge you with harassment," Franks snapped.

Deke gave him a menacing look, but didn't budge. "You lied to us when you claimed that no babies were lost at the manor. I saw a tiny grave today for myself. The one that belongs to Elsie's little girl."

Frank's wide brown eyebrows shot up. Surprise or was he faking his reaction?

"I didn't lie. I never took care of any deceased infants or children at that orphanage."

"You didn't perform an autopsy on her baby?"

Elsie shivered but stood her ground beside Deke, determined to get answers.

"No."

"Did Hodges tell you about the baby?"

"No. I never knew what happened. I assumed the child was adopted."

"What about Mires?" Deke pressed. "I can't imagine him not confiding in you."

"Maybe he was afraid he'd get busted, and he didn't want anyone who could testify against him."

"Are you sure you didn't know about my daughter?" Elsie pleaded. "I just want to know if I could have done something to have saved her."

Franks grimaced and turned away. "I'm sure Mires did everything possible for your child."

Elsie inhaled a deep breath. "He said she had the umbilical cord wrapped around her neck. That she wasn't breathing." The memory swept her back to the despair she'd felt that day. "He claimed he tried to revive her, but it was too late."

"I'm sorry," Franks said, a note of sincerity to his voice. "But sometimes things are beyond our control, Miss Timmons."

Elsie heard his words, but she couldn't accept them. If she'd taken better care of herself, run from Hodges before he'd gotten his hands on her, she might have saved her child's life. And nothing could ever convince her otherwise.

"What did they tell the family who'd already signed up to adopt my baby?"

"I'm the wrong person to ask these questions," Franks replied. "Perhaps you should speak to the social worker who handled your case."

"We intend to do that," Deke said. "Maybe she'll give us an honest answer."

Elsie hardened her heart to this man. She sensed he was lying, that he knew more about her baby than he'd admitted. And if she found out that was true, she and Deke would be back.

KNOWING ELEANOR hadn't always been stable, and that he had to inform her of her brother's death, Bush phoned her first, but there was no answer. Anxious as to how she'd react, and curious if she had killed Mires, he drove to her house, but the lights were off, the house bathed in darkness. He parked and climbed out, then strode up to the door anyway. Maybe she was asleep, her kids tucked safely in bed, the knot of anxiety yanking at his chest an overreaction.

She and Donna would not do something so stupid as to shoot the doctor. For God's sake, he was Eleanor's brother. She owed him.

He knocked on the door, then rang the doorbell but no one responded. They had to be asleep. The baby kept her up at night. She'd probably gone to bed early.

But still worry niggled at him, so he peeked through the glass in the garage window. It was empty. Damn. He'd hoped he'd find her and get the news over with. And he'd hoped she'd assure him that she hadn't been anywhere near Dr. Mires's office earlier. Now, he didn't know what to think.

He had to talk to Donna.

Leaves swirled on the ground in front of him as he rushed back to the car, the clouds obliterating the moon and stars, as if darkness had swallowed the sky forever.

Twelve years ago it had started. All when Hodges had opened that orphanage. He'd thought the night of the fire that that dark spell had ended.

But it hadn't. Over the years, the evil had festered like a sore rotting away the skin and eating at the soul of the people in town. The secrets. The lies. The town of the damned. No one came or stayed here without being scarred by its evil.

A pain ripped through his chest, and he inhaled sharply, massaging the knot of anxiety. He felt as if he was having a damn heart attack. Yanking open his glove compartment, he grabbed the aspirin bottle, uncapped it and tossed back an aspirin. Then he leaned over the steering wheel and heaved for a steadying breath, trying to calm himself while he punched in Donna's number. She didn't like it when he called her home, and he hoped to hell her old man wasn't around, but he had to see her.

She answered on the third ring. "Sheriff," she said in a low voice. "I thought you weren't going to call me at home."

"It's important. I have to see you. Now."

"What's going on?" she whispered.

"We'll talk when we meet. Is Billy Rae there?"

"Yes."

"Is he sober enough to watch the kid?"

"Yes, Carly's already gone to bed."

"Then make up an excuse to get out. I'll meet you at our regular place."

She hesitated. "Give me fifteen minutes."

He hung up, then drove through the foggy night toward the deserted cabin they used off Hardscrabble Road in the mountains. Anxiety to see Donna tonight, even if it was to question her, sent excitement through his veins. God, how he loved that woman. If only she'd leave Billy Rae....

He stopped to pick up a bottle of wine just in case she had time for some loving, then sped up the icy road. Five minutes later, he let himself in, started a fire and lit the kerosene lamp. Tucked away in the mountains near Satan's Falls, the cabin was surrounded by nature, a perfect place for their rendezvous. Trees hid their cars, just as they'd had to hide their feelings for the past few years.

A howl from somewhere in the forest echoed in the wind, and he thought of the ghosts and wild animals that surrounded them, the supposed werecats and bobcats, the devil. He should have moved away from here years ago like that social worker, Renee Leberman, had. Then he wouldn't be dealing with this crap now. And maybe Donna would have run away with him.

Her Toyota rumbled up the graveled drive, and he peeked outside to make sure no one had followed her. Seconds later, she rushed into the room, looking flushed and nervous.

"What's this about, Wally?"

He wanted to touch her, but first he had to know the truth. "Dr. Mires was murdered tonight."

She gasped and fidgeted with her coat.

"Donna, did you or Eleanor have something to do with this?"

Her face paled, and she sank down onto the faded sofa, the firelight flickering across her cheeks. "Why would you ask that?"

"I know you were with Eleanor this afternoon. I saw the two of you in town." He cleared his throat, hating to doubt her, but the need for the truth pushed him on.

"Tell me, Donna. Did the two of you kill him?"

Chapter Fourteen

"I want to talk to Renee Leberman tonight," Deke said as he and Elsie left the medical examiner's office.

Elsie tugged her coat tighter around her, wishing the brutal weather would relent. She couldn't remember when she'd seen the sun. Did it ever shine on this godforsaken mountain?

"It's time I faced her, too." Renee's job had been to protect them, not let them be used by a monster.

"Where does she live?" Elsie asked.

"Outside of Nashville." He traced a finger along her hand. "You look exhausted, Elsie. Why don't you grab a nap while I drive?"

Elsie slid deeper into the warmth of her coat and the car and closed her eyes. Deke was right. She was exhausted. Yet someone was still after her. Someone who wanted her dead.

Which meant that she and Deke had to be close to finding the truth about who wanted to keep her quiet.

Deke's fingers brushed her cheek. "Go on and relax. You're safe right now. I promise to take care of you."

Just this once, she closed her eyes and allowed Deke's words to assuage her worries. She *was* safe with him.

She yawned and snuggled closer to him. As she drifted to sleep, she wondered what it would be like to spend every night with him. Safe by his side. In his arms. Making love until dawn.

Never alone again.

DEKE CRADLED ELSIE to him the entire ride, savoring the feel of her body next to his, the sweet way she'd rested her hand on his chest. She was beginning to trust him. The mere thought ignited a thrill inside him. He stroked her hair, wanting this mess to be over with, so he could take her in his arms, make love to her and make her his.

His breath caught, the reality of his thoughts twisting his stomach. Yet, the fear that usually clawed at him at the thought of committing to a woman didn't come. Instead, a peace floated over him as if he was exactly where he belonged. The same kind of peace he felt in the woods or when he worked with the falcons.

Outside, the dark clouds persisted, but thankfully, the ice storm that had been predicted passed, so he made the drive in a short time. The small subdivision where Renee Leberman lived was tucked away from the heart of Nashville, but lay close enough to show the signs of country music. Billboards for new acts, the Grand Ole Opry and country-and-western dance clubs welcomed visitors to the town. He checked the address, followed the map to her house, then parked in the driveway.

He gently shook Elsie. "Wake up, sweetheart, we're here."

Elsie stirred, her hand falling to his lap, and he tensed. Half the ride he'd had an erection that had strained his jeans. Her hand only turned his body into agony.

She glanced up at him, then down to his lap, and realized what had happened. "Oh, sorry."

He fought a grin. She looked sleepy and tousled, as if she'd read his desire and felt it, too. The mere thought sent his heart racing with the need to have her, but he shifted, squeezed her hand, then removed it and laid it on the seat between them. A symbol of the distance they needed to keep, a symbol that he wanted her but would wait until the right moment. The promise he'd made, that he would have her one day, echoed in his mind. That day was near. "I need a minute before we go inside."

The faint smile of a woman who had let down

her defenses appeared, lighting up her gorgeous eyes, stealing his breath. He wanted to make her smile like that every day.

"You look beautiful, Elsie."

She blushed, and he forced his mind back on track. They had to question Renee Leberman, which meant Elsie had one more demon from her past to confront today.

She finger-combed her long wavy hair, then brushed lip gloss across her lips. He jerked his head to the side so he didn't have to watch, then studied the yard. Out back, he noticed a swing set and trampoline, indicating that Renee Leberman had a child. For a brief second, he entertained the idea that she had adopted a child from Wildcat Manor, and realized that there were probably other locals who'd done so ten years ago.

Any one of them might be trying to run Elsie out of town. Opening up the past meant exposure, that other girls might return in search of the children they had lost. He needed a list of all the deliveries and adoptions.

But Mires had probably shredded them all. Maybe Renee had kept copies.

"I'm ready," Elsie said, breaking into his thoughts.

He nodded, then climbed out and met Elsie at the front of the car. This time when he took her hand to pick their way up the snow-packed ground, she squeezed his hand in response. "Thank you for being here with me, Deke. I...don't know how to repay you."

They stepped onto the porch of the modest brick ranch. "You don't have to repay me, Elsie. I'm glad I'm here for you."

An odd tingle shot through him, then he broke eye contact and banged the duck-shaped door knocker.

An elderly woman opened the door slightly, the chain still intact.

"We're looking for Renee Leberman," Deke said.

The woman furrowed her thinning gray eyebrows. "Who are you?"

A petite girl about nine or ten years old poked her head under the woman's arm. "Who is it, Grandma?"

"I don't know, child. Go on and finish that cross-word puzzle."

"But I'm stumped." The little girl wrinkled a freckled nose. "I can't figure out six down or ten across."

"I'll be there to help you in a minute," the woman said. "Now, go back in the kitchen."

The child pouted, but did as she was told.

Deke saw the pained smile on Elsie's face, and knew she must be thinking of her own daughter. She would have been about the same age as the little girl, just like several of the children in town.

"Tell me who you are and what you're doing here," the woman demanded.

Deke straightened his shoulders, trying to understand her anger. "My name is Deke Falcon, and this is Elsie Timmons. Is Renee your daughter?"

The woman nodded, although her mouth pinched into a frown. "I don't talk to strangers," she said in a shaky voice.

"I'm not exactly a stranger," Elsie said. "I knew Miss Leberman years ago. She was a social worker who worked with me at an orphanage in Wildcat."

The woman started to slam the door, but Deke caught it with his boot. "What's wrong, ma'am? We just want to talk to Renee."

"That's what that fancy lawyer said when he came out here a few months ago, but two weeks later, they found my daughter dead."

Elsie gasped, and Deke gripped his hands by his side to stifle his frustration. "I'm sorry about your loss. What happened to her?" he asked in a quiet voice.

Tears filled the woman's eyes. "The local police said it was some freak accident, but…"

"But you don't think so?"

"No. Renee got really upset when that man showed up. She told me we might have to move, and that she was going to find us a new place. She was out looking when she had the accident."

"I'm so sorry," Elsie said in a strained voice. "I know you're devastated. And her little girl must be, too."

"That's the worst part," the woman said. "Renee never married. And now Allison will have to grow up without a mother."

Deke slid a hand behind Elsie's back, sensing how the comment must have affected her. But Renee's death meant a dead end for them, as well. Unless social services had information. It was worth a try.

"At least she has you," Deke said. "I'm sure you'll love her and give her a good home."

Not like the violent, abusive one where Elsie had grown up.

Deke cleared his throat. "What was the lawyer's name who came to see her?"

"I don't know." Her hands turned white as she gripped the door edge. "But I think he killed Renee."

ELSIE THOUGHT ABOUT the little girl and Renee Leberman while Deke drove them back toward Wildcat Manor. Although her grandmother seemed to care for Allison, Elsie hated that she had to go through life motherless.

Why had the lawyer come to see Renee? What had upset her? Could it possibly have been regarding the adoptions?

"Deke, do you think Burt Thompson might have been the one to visit Renee?"

Deke shrugged. "It's possible. I'm going to talk to the police in Nashville tomorrow. See what their investigation turned up."

"What if Renee had decided to come forward about the abuse at the orphanage?" Elsie suggested.

"That's a possibility, and her death seems too coincidental not to be related. But why would she do so now?" He scrubbed a hand through his hair, spiking the long ends, and Elsie half smiled, wanting to brush it down. But that gesture seemed so intimate. Maybe too forward....

"I don't know." Elsie chewed her lip.

"We have to be prepared. She might have simply had an accident," Deke said.

"Her mother certainly didn't seem to think so." Elsie gave in to temptation and finally brushed his hair with her fingers. Deke gave her an odd look, but heat flickered in his eyes.

"She did seem scared." He hesitated, then laid his hand over hers, threading their fingers together.

Elsie's imagination went wild as they neared the manor. "If Renee had planned to expose the truth, perhaps she talked to Hattie Mae. Maybe she even sent her a letter."

Deke considered her theory. "Then Thompson found out, and killed Renee to keep her quiet."

A horrid thought occurred to Elsie. "What if he killed Hattie Mae, too?"

Deke frowned. "That's possible—"

Deke never finished the sentence. Suddenly a black SUV roared up on his tail. He glanced up, but the vehicle slammed into his rear end with such force that his Range Rover spun out of control. He tried to brake, to turn the steering wheel into the spin, but the SUV hit him again on the driver's side, then sent him skidding toward the guardrail. Tires screeched. Elsie screamed and grabbed the armrest as they flipped and spun into a roll down the mountain ridge. He threw his arm forward to protect her from hitting the dash. The air bags deployed, filling the front and slamming them both back into the seat. A sharp pain hit his chest, and he assumed Elsie had felt one, too. That or worse. She was so small, the air bag might have broken her ribs. The vehicle bounced and shook as it rolled over the uneven rocky terrain. Metal screeched as it finally landed at the bottom of the ravine. Glass shattered.

No. They weren't at the bottom. Through the glass, he saw the bottom—they had landed on a ridge above it. His SUV teetered on the edge and might go over any second.

Panic forced Deke into action. "Elsie, are you all right?"

A strangled sob echoed from behind the air bag,

and he gently opened his door, not wanting to rock the SUV. The smell of gasoline filled the air. They had to get out before the gas tank exploded.

"Elsie, can you move?"

"I…I'm not sure."

"Try to open your door. Easy though." He yanked his pocketknife out, and cut through the air bag, then crawled through the doorway. He climbed out on the rocks, holding his breath as he circled the back of the vehicle to reach the passenger side.

The smell of gasoline grew stronger. Blood dribbled down his chin and his hand where glass had caught him. He fought panic. The Rover couldn't blow or tip over, not until he got Elsie out.

Every second counted. "Don't move!" he yelled to Elsie. "Be very still, but turn your head away. I have to chip away the glass so I can get you out."

"Okay." Her voice sounded weak. Tired. Scared to death.

But Elsie was a fighter. She had to hang on now.

He yanked a handkerchief from his pocket, wrapped it around his hand, then chiseled the fragmented glass from the edge of the window with his knife.

"Okay," he shouted. "Try to reach my hand."

She shoved and pushed at the air bag as he tore it away with the knife. Finally he saw her face, her beautiful face, and reminded himself she was still alive. She reached for his hand and the SUV wavered. She screamed, and he dragged her through the small opening. As soon as she hit the ground, the Rover went over the side. He clutched her to him as they watched it fall another few hundred feet. It hit the bottom with a loud crash, then exploded into flames.

"Oh, my God!"

He pressed her head to his chest and heaved a breath, his own heartbeat tripping in his chest. "Elsie, I don't know what I would have done if I'd lost you."

"It's okay, I'm fine."

He was shaking all over. He had almost been too late. Then he would have lost her forever.

No, he couldn't think about that.

"Deke—"

"Shh, just let me hold you."

She trembled against him, then reached up and kissed him. Every pent-up moment of passion and emotion he'd experienced since he'd seen her assaulted him again. He wanted to make love to her right then and there.

But he couldn't. They were both bleeding and shaken, and she needed rest.

He pulled away slightly. "I have to call for help."

Just as he removed his cell phone, a gunshot rang through the air. It hit the rock beside him, then another pinged to his left. He pushed Elsie's head down, then pulled her behind the rocks for cover.

Seconds later, a deep voice shouted, "You won't get away this time!"

Deke withdrew his gun and fired back, then grabbed Elsie's hand and they raced across the path up to the road. When they reached it, they darted into the woods.

But the shooter was right behind them.

Chapter Fifteen

Elsie's heart pounded as she and Deke ran through the woods to escape the shooter. Deke pulled her along, weaving them in and out of the thickets of trees as if he knew the forest well and instinctively sensed which direction to go.

"We're not too far from the manor," he said. "About a mile. Can you make it?"

"Yes. Do you think he's still behind us?"

He yanked her sideways into the entrance of a small cave, then pressed a finger to her lips to silence her. In the distance, the slap of tree limbs shattering cut through the quiet. A howl that sounded as if it came from a madman followed.

Elsie shivered and mouthed the words, "Is that him?"

Deke nodded, although the flutter of the hawks' wings above drew her eyes to the black sky. Behind her, somewhere from the cave, another noise startled her, and she glanced at Deke. He cocked his head to the side, then gestured for her to rise slowly. Some kind of wild animal must be inside the cave. Something that might be dangerous....

Was it one of the overgrown mountain lions or werecats that supposedly roamed the woods?

The air tightened in her lungs, but Deke rubbed his hand along her back as if to assure her he'd protect her. He gestured toward the right, and she followed him, noting that he barely made a sound as he glided effortlessly in the wild. The hawk guided Deke as if he was born from the forest himself.

Behind them, another sound disturbed the calm, and suddenly a loud roar echoed from deep in the woods. Seconds later, the shrill shout of a terrorized man followed.

Elsie thought she saw the shadow of a man near the cave they had just left. Then another shadow, some kind of creature that looked half man, half animal pounced toward the shooter.

She clutched Deke's arm. He stared at the sight in silence, his expression stoic but accepting. The image of a big bobcat or mountain lion filled the shadows, then it lunged toward the man. She could almost smell the bloodlust of the beast, hear its teeth gnashing, as if it had caught the scent of its next meal and was ready to devour it.

She forced away the image as Deke glanced into her eyes.

"We're safe now," he said in a low voice. "Let's go back to the house."

"What was that?" Elsie asked, wondering if the rumors about the haunted forest were true.

"He's protecting us," Deke said. "That's all you need to know."

She swallowed hard, then nodded, her hands shaking as she gripped his hand and let him guide her the rest of the way. But as they walked up to the door, she looked back at the woods. As a child, she had been terrified of the ancient stories and wild animals. She'd never once ventured inside those woods, thinking that if she did, death would greet her.

Yet the house had held the demons.

And tonight the forest creatures she had been so terrified of had saved her life.

The trembling that had overtaken her since the accident and shooting started slowly abating. A fleeting memory of the night she and Torrie had escaped the orphanage drifted back, and she froze, another memory erupting through the darkness that had become her life. That night she had sensed someone or something, an animal, maybe part human, had been following her. She'd also sensed it had been watching over her, that it had guided her to safety.

Was it possible that the shadowed creature was

the same one? Had he lived in the woods all these years, perhaps guarding the children instead of hurting them as Hodges had done?

SHERIFF BUSH PACED in front of the fireplace like a madman as he waited on Donna's answer. "I want the truth, Donna. I know you and Eleanor were half-crazy with worry about your kids." He shoved his hand over his head, the dull ache in his chest persisting. "Did you and Eleanor go to Mires's office and kill him?"

His lovely Donna's lips tightened, and she twined her hands together, a sure sign she was nervous.

"We went to his office," she admitted.

His patience was like a thread unravelling from a worn piece of fabric. "And?"

"We wanted to talk to him about the adoptions," she admitted. "Make sure he didn't release any names or information."

"And then what?"

"He promised us no one would ever know that our children were adopted," she continued, her voice rising in hysteria. "That he would adjust the records so that if the birth mothers ever searched for their children, they wouldn't find anything."

"And so far, he's kept that promise," Bush reminded her. "Did he say he was going to release the information now?"

"Not exactly, but his eyes…you could look into his eyes and see he had second thoughts."

"Ah, hell." He lowered himself to the edge of the hearth and rubbed at his chest. "Please tell me you didn't…"

"Eleanor had a .38," Donna said in a voice that sounded strained, faraway as if she was remembering something that had happened to someone else.

His patience unwound another inch. Part of him didn't want to hear. Wanted to walk out the door and not look back. The part that belonged to the badge he wore forced him to press for the truth. "That's the same caliber of gun that killed Mires. Who shot him, Donna?"

"I didn't," she said in a rush. "Honestly, Wally."

"So Eleanor killed him. But you were an accessory."

"No, Eleanor didn't kill him, at least not while I was there." She knelt in front of him, and clutched his hands. "I swear, Wally. Dr. Mires promised her our secrets were safe. And when we left, he was still alive."

The air that had been trapped in Bush's lungs whooshed out in relief. Donna wouldn't lie to him, would she?

No…he trusted her. And she knew he would have taken care of her, no matter what.

He arched a brow. "After that, you both left?"

She nodded. "I did, and Eleanor said she was going to do some errands in town."

Bush cursed. "But she could have gone back to his office and killed him after you left."

Donna's eyes widened in terror. "Oh, my stars, surely not. I know she was upset, scared to death actually, but there had to have been someone else. Eleanor couldn't kill her own brother."

"Who do you think did then?"

Donna ran a hand through her hair, mussing the ends, and he wanted to take her in his arms and soothe her worries.

"Maybe that Timmons girl," she whispered. "Or…I don't know. Burt Thompson. Or someone else who was afraid he'd reveal their secrets. Eleanor and I are not the only ones who adopted kids back then."

Bush met her gaze. What the hell was he supposed to do now? He was the sheriff. He had to investigate this crime. But if he did, the secrets of the past would likely be exposed.

Then all of them would be in trouble….

DEKE CONTEMPLATED PHONING the sheriff but didn't trust the man to help them. For all he knew, Bush might be involved with whoever had tried to kill them. After all, Bush hadn't wanted them in town and had tried to run them off with verbal threats and warnings.

"I want to check on the falcon," he said, hoping Elsie understood the unsettled feeling in his gut.

"Of course. I'll go with you."

He nodded, glad she'd offered since he didn't intend to be away from her for a second. They walked around back to the toolshed and pushed open the door. The cage was silent.

Elsie's breathing whispered behind him, and he removed the cover of the cage. The falcon made a small squawking sound, then tried to push to its feet. Although the bird wobbled, he looked stronger.

"Is he going to be okay?"

"It looks like he's recovering. I'm going to check his bandage." He pulled on gloves, then opened the cage and slowly bent and talked to the bird in a low voice. Elsie stood beside him, her eyes fixed on him as the falcon climbed onto his arm. He crooned to the falcon as he brought him from the cage and examined him. The bird arched its back, its regal, statuesque form stronger now, and Deke breathed a sigh of relief.

"How do you do that?"

Deke smiled. "Practice. And a connection with the animal." He offered her a small smile. "A lot of patience, too."

A blush stained her cheeks as if she understood his silent comparison.

"I like watching you with them," she said quietly. "Deke, in the woods back there. I'm still curious about that creature—it looked part animal, part man. What was it?"

His dark eyes bore into hers. "What do you think it was?"

"I don't know." She rubbed her hands up and down her arms, shivering. "I always thought rumors about that sort of thing were only gossip. Folklore."

"Some things border on the paranormal," Deke said. "We want life to be easy, to only accept what we can see and understand. But we must honor all of God's creatures."

He knew his intensity might scare her off. But this was who he was.

"I never believed in anything I couldn't see," Elsie said.

"You can't see love, Elsie. But you do believe it exists, don't you?"

Elsie contemplated his question. A month ago, she would have said no. Then, pain, anger and bitterness had dominated her life. But she'd seen Deke with the falcons. And his connection wasn't exactly tangible, either.

And now that she had met Deke, *she* had changed.

"Elsie?"

"Yes, Deke." She smiled, and he brushed her face with the back of his hand. "I see love in your eyes when you talk about your family, and when you handle the falcons."

"And when I look at you," he said softly. "You see it then, too, don't you?"

Elsie bit down on her lip. She wanted to believe that was true so badly that her defenses cracked another notch.

"I know that I want to be with you tonight," Elsie whispered. "That my body gets hot and tingly when you look at me like that. That I trust you."

"And?"

She smiled. Earlier they had almost died. Then they'd run for their lives. She didn't want to miss another opportunity to hold Deke and be close to him. "I want to make love to you."

A hungry look darkened Deke's dark eyes, then a sultry smile tilted his lips. Unsated hungers rose within her. A need she desperately wanted to fill.

He turned and placed the falcon inside the cage, left it food and water, then removed his gloves and took her hand. "Let's go inside, Elsie. Then I'll show you what love is. Even if you can't see it, I want you to feel it."

DEKE'S HEART WAS BEATING so fast he could barely breathe. He wanted to prove to Elsie everything she meant to him, that a man could be gentle, but loving, yet his need for her pulsed so strongly through him that he feared he couldn't be gentle. That the wild animal and primal male inside him would come unleashed and he'd take her hard and fast and raw.

When they entered the manor, he paused to listen, then searched the entire house. Today's call had been too close for him to let down his defenses. They had almost been killed earlier. That thought alone spiked fear and adrenaline, along with the conviction that he had to hold Elsie and make love to her. What if he'd died and never had the chance?

Elsie followed him through the house quietly, and he led her back to the bedroom. He took her hands in his and looked into her eyes. A small streak of fear still lay in the depths, but desire also flared. "It's been an ordeal tonight. Are you sure you're all right? You didn't get hurt in the accident?"

"No, I'm okay."

"The air bag?"

She smiled. "Okay, maybe I'm a little sore, but really, Deke, I'm fine."

He pressed a soft kiss to her parted lips. "Why don't you get a shower while I lock up downstairs."

She nodded. "Or…you could join me when you come back up."

Surprised by her comment, he searched her eyes to make certain she meant the offer, then leaned over and kissed her cheek, her ear, then her mouth again. "All right."

She bit her lip, turned and headed to the bathroom with a smile. He watched her hips sway seductively, then rushed down the steps, locked all the doors, checked the windows, then grabbed two candles from the den and hurried back to her.

The furnace rumbled, the familiar squeaks and groans of the house echoing in the chilly air as she stepped into the bathroom. Still wearing her clothes, Elsie stared into the mirror. He set the candles on the vanity and lit them, then flipped off the light.

"Deke?"

He moved up behind her. "We don't have to do this if you've changed your mind." His fingers trembled as he reached up to stroke her hair away from her neck.

Emotions played on her face, evident in her reflection in the mirror. "No, I want this very much," she whispered.

"Any time, if you want me to stop, just say so," he whispered.

She nodded, and he kissed the nape of her neck, then slid his hands down to her waist and lifted her sweater over her head. She raised her arms and watched him undress her in the mirror, a sultry expression darkening her eyes. Next he unbuttoned her shirt slowly, planting a kiss on each inch of her delicate throat, neck and then lower until she stood wearing only a pale blue bra and jeans. His breath caught at the sight of her breasts spilling over the edges. Her winter clothes had disguised the size of her breasts and her slender abdomen. He kissed the curve of her breasts, then teased her nipples to firm peaks with his fingers through the bra. Her breath quickened as he unsnapped the garment, and it fell to the ground. She exhaled, making her chest rise and the dark tips of her nipples strain toward him.

He couldn't stand the anticipation. He lowered his head and licked the tip of each one, then closed his mouth over her right breast and suckled her gently. Inflamed by her, his hunger grew. His sex throbbed against his jeans, and he pulled back, suckled the other breast, while his fingers trailed down to unfasten her jeans. She gripped his shoulders, her body quaking.

Raw passion made him impatient. They had to shower before he took her standing up against the cold tile wall.

Not what he wanted for the first time. Not what she deserved.

Forcing himself to withdraw slightly, he glanced up and saw the look of pleasure and anticipation in her eyes and smiled, then opened the shower door and set the spray of water. She helped him shuck her jeans, then stood in a pair of silky blue thong panties that made his chest ache. He'd never seen anything so beautiful. She mesmerized him.

He started unbuttoning his shirt, but she surprised him by taking over the task. Each time she touched him, fire rippled through him. Her breath brushed his cheek as she pushed his shirt off, and his sex surged even harder. She kissed his jaw, ran her tongue along his neck then kissed his flat nipples. Lower her tongue bath went, all the way to his belly. He sucked in a sharp breath, his pulse pounding. His body ached, and only she could assuage the pain.

He wanted to love her until she was mindless with pleasure.

Adrenaline pumping, he lifted her face gently and kissed her mouth, then shook his head. "I... we'd better get in the shower."

A wicked smile tilted her lips, and she nodded, as if she'd known exactly what she'd accomplished with her teasing.

He slid off his boxers, half afraid his size would frighten her, and she'd ask him to stop. Instead her eyes widened, darkening with hunger. She reached out to touch him, but he slid her hand away, and shook his head. "Not yet."

Sinfully aroused, he caught the edges of her panties and pushed them down her slender thighs, exposing the heart of her. Her sharp intake of air pleased him, and she quivered when he kissed her belly. Her skin felt like satin, her body soft, all woman. Knowing he was about to come unraveled, he coaxed her into the shower. He took the sponge, soaped it and began to bathe her, starting with her neck, then brushing it over her arms and chest and her breasts.

"That feels wonderful," she whispered. "I've... never done this before."

He grinned. "I want to make you feel good, Elsie. Special." He kissed one rosy hard tip. "Loved."

She blushed faintly, but allowed him to turn her around and wash her back, her spine, then lower until his hands cupped her rear. He forgot the sponge then, simply lathered his hands and stroked them over her backside, down her legs, then parted them slightly until he bathed her essence. She moaned softly, and he turned her around to face him, knelt and stroked her from the front, wetting and soaping the dark curls that protected her femininity. Mesmerized by her womanhood, he memorized every inch of her.

Finally he delved into her folds, stroking her with his soapy fingers until she clutched his shoulders, threw her head back and groaned. The water washed the bubbles down her neck and chest and he stood, lowered his head and kissed her breasts, once again suckling each one, while his fingers stroked between her thighs. Her tiny moans and erratic breathing coaxed him to continue, and his hunger built as he suckled her nipples harder, more urgently. Desire pulsed through him so intense, he thought he'd explode just from listening to her erotic sounds. But he tamped down his own need and slid one finger inside her, then another. She clutched at his arms and shoulders, hanging on as if she'd collapse if he released her.

He continued to fill her with his fingers, using his thumb to stroke the bud of her desire. Suddenly she threw her head back and cried out his name. Her body spasmed around his fingers, and he smiled, deepening the pressure, sucking her harder, pushing his fingers to the hilt as she whimpered her orgasm.

When he finally felt the tremors subsiding, he kissed her mouth, slowing his movements, until she opened her eyes and looked at him. The euphoria shining in her expression made his chest swell and his body surge with need.

"Deke—"

"Shh," he whispered. "We're not finished."

She nodded. "Now I want to bathe you."

He swallowed hard at her sultry look, his sex jutting toward her, another wave of heat assaulting him. He didn't know how much torture he could stand, but he handed her the sponge. Their gazes locked and he memorized her face, her eyes, those tantalizing lips.

He wasn't the same man he was when he'd met her.

Hell, he'd lost all objectivity.

But he would leave her when the time came.

Go back to his job.

It was the way it had to be.

And he'd live with it.

Chapter Sixteen

Elsie's body tingled all over from Deke's touch. She had never known anything so erotic. She wanted more, wanted to taste and explore him, wanted him inside her, filling her, heating her blood, loving her, making her whole again.

The strength of her emotions frightened her.

Yet it excited her at the same time.

She had to be in love with Deke. She'd never felt this intense need for another man. She couldn't survive another day without knowing this exquisite physical pleasure.

Determined to equal his passionate exploration, she soaped the sponge, then stroked it over his arms slowly, washing each corded ripple of his chest and torso. The water and bubbles swirled in the water, washing over his dark chest hair, his flat stomach and lower to his sex where it jutted out, full and hard. She had never seen a man so large, and ached to wrap her hands around his thick length, but decided to torture him a while longer. While she washed his chest and stomach, he raked her hair over one shoulder, then watched her, the tight set to his mouth as he breathed indicating he liked her touch and didn't want her to stop. She didn't intend to.

Smiling playfully, she stared at his sex blatantly for a moment, then flipped him around so she could wash his back. He surprised her by leaning forward with his hands on the wall, giving her a magnificent view of his firm, muscled back, shoulders, thighs and hips. Her breath hitched at the power in his body, yet she'd experienced his tenderness, as well, and fear faded from her thoughts. There was no room for it here, not between them.

She did as he had done, dropped the sponge, and soaped her hands instead, running them over his neck, his back, across his shoulders and down his arms, then trailing them down his spine until she reached his waist. She let them slip over his hips, but only slightly, and saw him tense, then washed his legs, savoring the feel of his muscular thighs and calves as she touched them. Finally, she ran her fingers up his legs to his waist, then soaped them again and splayed her hands over his buttocks. Her heart pulsed faster as he hissed a response that sounded almost painful.

"Elsie, you have no idea what you're doing to me."

A wave of uncertainty flashed over her. "I... want to please you. I know I'm not experienced, though—"

He spun around so fast she gasped. His eyes glazed with arousal, and he gripped her arms. "You may think I do this all the time, but I don't. It's been a long time, and even then, it wasn't like this." He kissed her firmly, hungrily. "It was never like this."

"Deke—"

"Shh. All you have to do is look at me and it makes me hard. Your touch sets me on fire. It's pure torture." He brushed his fingers over her chin.

Her heart soared, and her mouth moved to say the words she felt in her heart, but for some reason, they lodged in her throat. He didn't hesitate, though. He kissed her again, and she melted in his arms. Her hand slid down, the need to touch his throbbing length driving her mad, and she cupped his erection in her hand and stroked his pulsing member. He moaned in his throat, thrusting forward so they were so close the tip of him brushed against her sex. She parted her legs, wanted him closer.

He drew back slightly, then turned off the water, and reached for a towel. "I want you in the bed. Now."

Exhilarated by his commanding voice, she nodded. She felt wanton, heathen, but she didn't care. She wanted him to take her so badly her knees nearly buckled.

He dried himself quickly, then took the other towel and dried her, patting places no man had touched in ages. With a low growl, he lifted her in his arms and carried her to the bed, flipped down the coverlet and laid her on the sheets. Firelight flickered across his face, the edge to his eyes almost predator-like, possessive and all consuming.

She ran her hand down his chest again, then southward to his sex. "I didn't get to finish touching you."

"Later," he said on a groan. Then he threw her back on the bed, climbed over her and cupped her face in his hands. His lips devoured her, his tongue sent lazy sweet licks along her neck, her nipples, then more hungrily as he suckled her breasts again. She bucked upward, aching for him to fill her now, ready to take him inside her, but he continued to torment her. Finally, when she thought he was going to enter her, he crawled between her thighs, lowered his head and tasted the heart of her. She cried out in protest, wanted him inside her, then felt his wet moist tongue licking her folds. She whimpered and dug her hands into his arms, unsure if she could take any more teasing. But he pushed her legs farther apart, slid his tongue inside and made suckling noises as he fed on her.

Waves of excitement crashed back and forth in her body, rising and ebbing like the tides, then finally erupting into a thousand brilliant shades of color. She trembled all over, whispering his name, begging, pleading for him to come inside her.

When she thought she might die from not having him, he suddenly moved over her, shoved her legs wider with his knee and settled his hard length against her opening.

"Deke, please…"

His dark smile made her gasp, then he watched her eyes as he slid on a condom and slowly pushed himself inside her. She'd known he was big, had anticipated the feel of him stretching her, but nothing could have told her how erotic and mind changing having him throbbing inside her heat could be. He paused, apparently giving her body time to adjust, and she cried out again. "Please, Deke, I want you. More of you. All of you."

His breath hissed out, then he lowered his mouth and kissed her. Wild with sensations and need, she grabbed his hips and clutched his backside, urging him to move deeper, harder, faster. He braced his hands beside her, and thrust again, then slowly withdrew, rubbing her center with the tip of his sex, teasing her again and again until the delicious sensations overwhelmed her. Her body quivered helplessly, and she bucked upward, pulling him back inside her aching center. He groaned and moved his hips in a slow circle, embedding his full length into her, then building the rhythm slowly until he gained momentum.

Sweat beaded on his chest, and his arms shook with the force as the tension built to a crescendo. Her breath rushed out in small pants, and he slapped their bodies together, thrusting in and out until their bodies became one. Faster, harder, deeper, faster, harder, deeper. Her chest was about to explode. Erotic pleasure rushed over her, another wave of spasms rippling through her. With her release, he lowered his mouth, caught her moan, then thrust one more time, burying himself so deeply that she felt the connection all the way to her bones. A connection she wanted forever.

He threw his head back, his muscles clenching, and stared into her eyes. A second later, a roar ripped from his gut as he poured himself inside her.

Deke trembled all over from the force of his release, the warmth of Elsie's loving body below him a memory he'd savor the rest of his life. He also wanted to prolong the pleasure and hold her forever.

If he moved, she might have regrets and push him away. He'd never put his heart and soul on the line for a woman before. He wasn't even sure how it had happened this time. He sure as hell hadn't meant to.

She traced her fingers up and down his back, and he realized he might be smothering her, so he rolled them to the side, still holding her in his arms so their bodies were wound together.

He brushed a kiss on the top of her head, then threaded his fingers through her hair. "Are you okay, Elsie?"

A small giggle escaped her, then she looked up into his eyes, and his heart melted again.

"I'm wonderful," she whispered against his chest. "I…I've never felt that with anyone else."

And she damn well wouldn't ever again. He bit back the comment, then tilted her chin up and kissed her. "I don't want to ever let you go."

Tears moistened her eyelashes, but she blinked them away, then curled into his arms and rested her head against his chest. His heartbeat picked up. "I want this night to last forever."

He smiled for a minute, then frowned, wondering at her statement. Did she mean that tonight would be their only night together? No.

He forgot the question, though, as Elsie nibbled on his chin again. He didn't want to talk anyway. He wanted to make love to her over and over until she realized that she would never be able to leave him….

THE TIME HAD COME to finish Elsie Timmons. And that man…Falcon. He wanted to kill him, but he'd done his homework and learned Falcon had two brothers who worked with him. They'd probably come hunting for his killer if he died, and *he* would never have peace.

He pulled the cloak snugly around him and raised the hood that shielded his ugliness from the world, hating that he had to live in the shadows. The devil, they called him. The little kids ran. The women screamed in horror.

Only a while longer…then he would be free. Free of the ghosts that had haunted him ever since Hattie Mae had died….

Damn her.

Why had she given that house to the Timmons girl? Just to punish him.

She was the one who deserved punishment, to rot in her grave for her betrayal.

Formulating a plan in his mind, he struggled against the wind as he weaved through the forest. The storm that threatened loomed dark and ominous, and the first cackle of thunder rent the air, lightning zigzagging across the tops of the mountain ridge, the scent of its wrath scorching the air.

Darkness cloaked Wildcat Manor, the absence of light telling him that Elsie and Falcon were asleep. Now was the perfect time to strike.

A wicked grin lifted the corner of his mouth as he imagined his hands tightening around Elsie's throat, and the look of terror on her face when she realized that she was going to die. To think, that she had run from the manor to escape her sins. Yet she had never really escaped them, no matter how hard she'd tried.

Now he would make her his before she died....

THE STORM RAGED OUTSIDE, snapping tree limbs and sending them banging against the windows and the roof. Elsie jerked fully awake. Deke stirred beside her, his arms firmly around her. She felt so safe in his arms, but the storm's fury rattled the window-panes and the fire had gone out during the night, pitching them in darkness. A loud boom sounded as if an electrical pole had been hit by lightning, then another loud boom. Maybe a tree falling?

"Deke?"

"I'm here." He pressed a kiss to her lips, then sat up and felt for the light switch. When he flicked it, nothing happened.

"The storm must have blown out the generator," Elsie said, shivering from the chill in the room.

"I'll go check," Deke said. He stood and Elsie saw his naked body highlighted by a streak of light-ning and her heart throbbed.

"Deke?"

"Yeah?" He grabbed his jeans and yanked them on.

God, his voice was so gruff yet tender. "Thank you for last night."

He paused and turned to her, then leaned over the

bed and cupped her face in his hands. "That was only the beginning. I'll be right back." He took her gun from the end table and laid it beside her. "Use this if you need to."

The sight of the gun destroyed the simmering memory of their lovemaking and reminded her of their earlier close call with death.

He checked his own weapon, then stepped out of the bedroom. The stairs squeaked as he descended, the never-ending fear swallowing her as he moved farther and farther from her side.

What if someone was in the house and turned off the lights as a trap?

Nerves skittered through her as she waited. Maybe the person who'd tried to run them off the road had followed them here? He was probably the same one who'd tried to kill her before. He knew exactly where she lived.

What if he hurt Deke?

Tension drew her shoulders back and fired her senses. She slipped on her robe, tightened the belt, then clutched her gun in her right hand. Bracing herself for a fight, she tiptoed to the door, pausing to listen. Something rattled in the basement. Thunder added to the tension, rain pounded the roof. The wind's shrill whistle sent a chill down her spine.

She stepped into the hallway and scanned the

dark interior, but suddenly the whisper of a breath brushed her neck.

The scent of oil, smoke and sandalwood engulfed her. She froze, memories interrupting her rational thoughts. He was here. She knew it.

The man who'd sent her fleeing the manor in terror. The man who'd brutalized and terrorized and killed the young girls.

The man she'd killed.

No, it couldn't be. It was his ghost. That or someone was driving her crazy.

Her fingers tightened on the gun, and she pivoted, but suddenly a hand clamped down over her mouth and another one gripped her around the neck.

"Scream or fight me, and your lover boy dies."

DEKE HAD THE FEELING that something bad was about to happen.

He always trusted his instincts, but in this case, he had no idea if the trouble he sensed was due to the past day's events, to the danger following Elsie or to the fact that he'd made love to her and that he expected any second for her to run away.

For God's sake, man, get a grip. If she doesn't want you, hell, you can take her back to her mother's and walk away. Reuniting her with her mother was your job.

Sleeping with her hadn't been part of the bargain.

He cursed at the darkness and slanted the flashlight across the basement, his skin crawling at the sight of the walls ripped apart, and the memory of finding the girls' bodies. Hodges had killed those girls, but who was trying to kill Elsie?

As he crossed the room to find the fuse box, he contemplated the suspects so far. Mires had been one of them—but now he was dead. Renee Leberman had also died, a suspicious death according to her mother.

The sheriff and the lawyer in town had reputations to uphold and would definitely want to cover up the past if it meant exposing them as possible accessories to abuse, murder and perhaps an illegal adoption ring. The coroner had denied that any babies or children had ever died at the center, but he had lied. Of course, there was the possibility that Hodges had covered up the deaths and the coroner hadn't known.

He was still going in circles.

He finally located the fuse box and quickly corrected what he thought might be the problem, but the lights remained off. Hmm. Maybe someone had had an accident and hit a power line or transformer. If so, it would take time to repair it.

Not wanting to leave Elsie for long, he turned to head back upstairs but a shadow from the back room caught his eye, and a scraping sound punctuated the eerie quiet. A second later he opened the door, and his pulse hammered.

The sheriff dangled from a rope attached to the ceiling, his body limp like a rag doll, his eyes glazed open in death.

The toes of his shoes scraped the steel table below him as he swung back and forth.

Chapter Seventeen

Reality sent Elsie spiraling into utter shock. This couldn't be happening.

He could not have survived. Not that horrendous fire....

And if he had, how and why had Hattie Mae kept his survival a secret?

"Yes, it's me," he said in that low coarse breath that had always nauseated her. "I'm back from the dead."

"But...how?" Elsie squeaked out.

"That's not important. What matters now is you and that detective." He leaned so close she felt his cheek against her hair. "Do you want me to kill him?"

A tremor ran through Elsie. She was in love with Deke. "No, God, no, please. I'll...do anything you say."

His bitter laugh rumbled out. "Then write him a goodbye note." He pushed her back into the room, then tossed a pad and pen on the desk by the door.

Elsie's hand trembled as she dropped into the chair. He kept the gun pointed at her head, and threw her revolver on the bed and out of reach. "What do I say?" Elsie stammered.

"Whatever you have to, to keep him from following us."

Elsie struggled for words. Deke was hardheaded, driven, would not give up easily. He'd put himself on the line for her. She couldn't let him die because of her. She'd never forgive herself.

But he wouldn't give up the case. Not and leave her mother without answers. Not and leave her… or would he?

His heart and body…that was it. She had to lie. Tell him she didn't want to be with him. Her fingers worked of their own accord, quickly scribbling the message on the page. All lies, but also words to protect him.

Words that would seal her fate.

But living with his death on her conscience would be worse than death itself. Besides, Hodges would kill her anyway. Maybe by saving Deke she could rest in peace with honor attached to her name, not the evil that had tainted her all her life.

He snatched the pen from her as soon as she finished, then jerked her arm. "Come on, Elsie. It's time you and I got reacquainted."

She shivered, wondering if she could fight him

off. But better wait until she got out of the house. Until Deke was safe.

He led her down the back stairway through the closet in the dorm room. Deke had nailed it shut, but he had already ripped away the nails. Probably while they'd been gone today. Seconds later, he dragged her through the rain and thunder into the woods. Her bare feet slapped across mud, stones and twigs as he shoved her into her car. He held her car keys in his hand and ordered her to drive.

Summoning her courage, she glanced sideways, but the dark hood shielded his face, the black night offering only a faint outline of his shape. Then he turned his head sideways and a flash of lightning illuminated the purple and red scars on his cheek. His left eye drooped, the skin around it mangled and discolored. Hatred and the madness of a killer lurked in his eyes.

"You like what you did to me, Elsie? You turned me into a monster."

Her heart pitched. "You were a monster before. You hurt all those girls, murdered some of them—"

He aimed the gun at her face. "Shut up and drive, you bitch."

Her fingers shook as she turned the key. The engine roared to life, a deafening sound that punctuated the tension thrumming through her body. She squeezed the steering wheel with clammy palms, knowing the minute she pressed the gas pedal, the car would take her farther and farther from the man she loved.

And into the lethal hands of a killer.

DEKE RACED UP THE STEPS from the basement, the dark house making it almost impossible to see, but he had to get to Elsie. If the man who'd killed Sheriff Bush was still in the house, he might go after her.

Before he reached the second floor, the sound of an engine cut into the night. He raced to the front door, threw it open and saw Elsie's car barreling down the drive. What the hell? Was Elsie driving? Was she alone in the car?

Or did the killer have her?

Panic gnawed at his throat as he jogged up the steps to the second floor, yelling her name. "Elsie! Elsie, are you here?"

He threw open the door to the bedroom, praying she was still in bed waiting for him, but the room was empty. The sheets were rumpled, their towels draped in the bathroom where they'd left them. But nothing else was disturbed.

He spotted the note on the desk, and frowned, then picked it up and recognized Elsie's handwriting.

Dear Deke,
  I can't take living in this town anymore. Being with you is smothering me. Tell my

mother I'll come home someday, but not now. And tell her that I love her.

Please don't follow me. I need to be alone and on the road just like my father.

Elsie

For a second, Deke simply stared at the scribbled words, a sharp pain jabbing at his chest. *He was smothering Elsie. She needed to be alone, away from him.*

Emotions twisted inside him, ripping him apart. He'd known that making love to her would change things. Had hoped it would bring them closer. And it had in his mind. He'd thought she'd felt it, too.

But obviously the feelings were one-sided.

Trying to dam the emotions rolling through him, Deke fell back on his anger.

He'd be fine without her.

But damn it, he'd promised Deanna he'd bring her daughter home, and he never went back on a promise. Besides, Elsie was in danger.

And he'd screwed up by making love to her, by frightening her so badly that she'd run off without a care for her own safety.

The image of the sheriff's body dangling from the rope in the basement seared his conscience again, and he jerked himself from his stupor. Someone had been in the house. A killer.

What if he'd gotten to Elsie? What if he'd made her write the note? What if he was with her?

He crumpled the note and threw it on the floor. When it hit the rug, he noticed a footprint impression. He knelt and felt the carpet. It was wet. A bootprint. Slightly muddy around the edges.

Damn it. The killer *had* been in here. And he had Elsie.

Fear screamed in his head, and he ran for the door, then realized he didn't have a car. He couldn't call the sheriff, either, because he was dead, but he'd call some locals.

He stumbled through the room to the nightstand and found his cell phone, then punched the number for his old friend, FBI Agent William Thurman, in Nashville. Thurman was helping his brother Brack track down Elsie's father.

"Agent Thurman."

"Will, it's Deke Falcon. I need your help."

"Is this about the Timmons woman?"

"Yes."

"I found her father. I was just about to fax a report to Brack."

"Where is he?"

"He's dead, Deke. Died in an alcohol-related accident five years ago."

He'd deserved something even more painful. "Listen, I need you to come and get me." He explained the circumstances. "I'll fill you in on everything else when you get here. But bring a crime scene unit with you. The local sheriff is dead in the basement."

Thurman hissed. "Let the nearest local cops know and I'll be there in about twenty minutes."

God, twenty minutes. Elsie might be dead by then. No, he couldn't think that way. She was strong, a fighter. She would make it through this. And he would take her home to Deanna.

Then he'd leave her alone and give her all the space she needed.

TEN MILES. Elsie had counted them, studied the directions, tried to memorize the route they'd taken in case she had a chance to escape. Chilled from the cold air seeping into the car and with fear gripping her, she clutched the terry cloth robe to her neck as she parked in front of the old cabin Hodges had forced her to drive to. She'd wound through several smaller dirt side roads until they were hidden so far back into the woods, no one would ever find her.

Despair threatened to rob her sanity, but she fought it. Just as it had been when she'd lived on the streets, she had to depend on herself if she was going to make it out of this mess alive. She'd done things she wasn't proud of in order to survive. She would do so again if it meant escaping Hodges. And this time, she'd expose all his dirty little secrets and make him pay by going to jail.

He shoved the gun in her side. "Get out, and don't try to run or I'll shoot you in the back."

Fear reared its ugly head, memories of her years at Wildcat Manor crashing back. But they hadn't destroyed her then, at least not completely. She'd met Deke, learned to trust again, even thought she might have a future with him.

Those bad memories couldn't hold her prisoner anymore. No, she would use them to fuel her anger, make her stronger, help her win the battle between good and evil.

Her bare feet stung as she stepped onto the icy ground, but she swallowed back the pain and forced her feet to move. Hodges yanked his cape around his shoulders, shoved the gun in her back and walked behind her, the sound of his labored breathing drilling the tension deeper inside her body. She took calming breaths, formulating a plan.

Go inside the cabin, scope it out for a weapon. Play it cool. Stall. Strike when you get the chance.

The rain slashed her cheeks, the wind tossing her hair around her eyes. He opened the door and she stepped inside, the instant heat of a wood-burning stove filling the room. Except for a bed, chair and a small scarred wooden table, the room was almost bare.

"See how you forced me to live?" Hodges grunted. "Like an animal."

He *was* one, she wanted to say, but refrained, knowing she'd only rile his temper. "Tell me why you hurt those girls," she whispered. "Miss Hattie Mae loved you at one time."

"She failed me," he snarled. "And the girls were so tempting. They asked for it by being sluts."

"They needed guidance and love," Elsie argued. "And Hattie Mae deserved better."

Anger reddened his discolored face, making the scars even more prominent. "She was going to betray me at the end," he growled. "She wanted to tell everyone I was still alive. That I had abused those girls, but I only gave them the punishment they deserved."

Elsie's heart thumped wildly. "You killed Hattie Mae, didn't you?"

He stepped closer to her, so close she smelled his fetid breath. His body also reeked, as if he hadn't bathed in days. "She shunned me after the fire, threatened to expose me if I ever returned to the manor. Then she took the girls away. And at the end, she grew a conscience." His depraved voice thundered through the room. "She had to die."

He was truly mad, Elsie realized. Completely demented.

"Why did everyone cover for you?" Elsie demanded.

His laughter shot through the dark room. "Because they wanted the babies," he said. "The doctor adopted one, then took one for his sister and the sheriff arranged one for his girlfriend, Donna. Even that social worker lady who thought she was so high and mighty adopted one." His hideous laughter reverberated through the room. "Ain't it amazing the price some people will pay to get a kid?"

He twisted a strand of her hair around his finger, and Elsie's knees grew weak, nausea climbing to her throat.

"You know, Elsie, I always wanted you. And it's been a long time for me." His sinister smile revealed yellowed teeth.

A cold sick dread washed over her. She would not let him touch her, not after knowing the sweet, loving touch of a real man. She'd rather die first.

He inched closer, the gun dropping to his side, and she seized the moment. She jabbed her nails at his scarred face, and he bellowed in rage. She threw her foot up, and kicked him in the face, then turned and ran. He fired the gun, but the bullet pinged off the floor near her feet, and she ran out the door. Rain splattered her face and body as she tore down the steps. She jumped in the car, but he'd taken the keys.

God, what now? She couldn't wait!

Frantic, she climbed out and ran toward the woods. His shout rang out behind her, and another shot pinged off the ground. The third one caught her ankle and sent her flailing to the ground. Pain ripped through her foot and ankle. She tried to get up, but he caught her by the hair then jammed the gun into her back again.

She held her breath, knowing she was going to die.

DEKE AND THURMAN RUSHED to the lawyer's office, but Thompson's desk looked as if it had been packed up, and he was moving out. He wasn't at home, either, so Thurman issued an APB, and alerted the airports, buses and train stations nearby.

"Almost everyone connected with the orphanage is dead," Deke said in frustration. "Let's try the coroner. He lied before about deaths at the manor. Maybe he knows more."

Five minutes later, they cornered the man at the morgue.

"I told you I didn't autopsy any infants."

"All that means is that Hodges buried the baby without one," Deke snapped. "Now, who has been trying to kill Elsie?"

The man rubbed sweat off his forehead. "Dr. Mires and Burt Thompson were aware of the adoptions and assisted Hodges. Dr. Mires was really a nice man. He sincerely wanted to help the girls, and his sister, Eleanor, desperately wanted a baby, so he arranged the adoption. Before he knew it, he was in so deep, he couldn't get out."

"And the sheriff?"

"The same. He helped Donna. But I don't think he knew about the murdered girls in the basement. Hodges hid things up there pretty well."

"How about you?"

"I told you the truth."

"Then who the hell is covering things up? And who killed Mires and the sheriff? Did Thompson do it?"

Franks glanced at the equipment in the autopsy room. "I'm not sure."

Deke jerked him by the collar. "You're keeping something from us, and if you don't tell me now, I'm going to lock you up."

"I swore to Hattie Mae, I'd never tell—"

Deke tightened his hands into a choke hold. "Tell what?"

Franks's eyes bulged. "That Hodges didn't die the night of the fire."

"What?"

"He was burned severely, and spent a long time in a rehab hospital. I fixed it so he was a John Doe.

Hattie Mae shut down the center, and promised him she wouldn't reveal that he was alive as long as he left her alone for the rest of her life."

"Where has he been all this time?" Deke asked.

"There's a deserted cabin in the woods, not too far from Wildcat Manor."

Deke shot Thurman a desperate look. "Elsie's worst nightmare, Hodges. My guess is he's got her now."

His blood ran cold as Franks gave him directions, then he and Thurman sprinted to the car to find her.

A few minutes later, they'd located the cabin, but no one was inside. The gunshot in the floor, a man's muddy bootprints that matched the ones in the orphanage and another set of footprints confirmed his suspicions. The woman's feet were bare.

Elsie's. Dear God, what had he done to her?

"Her car's still outside. They must be on foot," Thurman said.

Deke nodded. "Let's go."

As they jogged into the woods, a gunshot rent the air. Panic zinged through Deke as he raced toward it.

Elsie had to be alive….

HODGES DRAGGED ELSIE deeper into the bowels of the forest. It was so pitch-dark, she couldn't see his face, only the shadow of his black cape billowing behind him as he hauled her away from the cabin. She glanced through the dense foliage, wondering if the creature that had saved her and Deke might resurface.

"Where are we going?" Elsie shouted.

He yanked her harder. "Satan's Falls."

Of course. He was the devil reincarnate.

She panted for air, her lungs throbbing, her ankle aching. Blood streamed down to the ground, creating a crimson pool. A wild animal howled in the distance. An owl hooted. And the brush near them rustled with the sounds of a pack of wild dogs. He fired a shot at the animals, then shot again and again into the bushes.

She was going to die tonight. At the very hands of the man who had stolen part of her life.

No. She had to fight him. She had a chance with Deke. If she got loose, maybe one of the wild dogs or bobcats would attack Hodges.

He paused, brushing his forehead. His hood slipped down. Lightning struck nearby, and he turned to look at her. She gasped at the full view of his scarred, ugly face. Red, pocked, purplish skin that had been burned away and could never be replaced. But it was the vicious look in his eyes that terrified her the most. He was a man without a soul.

Thunder clapped above her, and the wind whirled leaves at her clothes and legs. He reached back his hand as if to slap her, but she kicked and lashed out at him instead. He loosened his grip for just a second, and she shoved free, then fled into the night as fast as she could.

But he was on her tail. She felt his footsteps, his cold searing eyes, his hand as he snatched her hair and dragged her to the ground. Then he tore at her like one of the wild animals from the woods. She screamed and bit at him, kicking violently and struggling to reach a tree limb or something for a weapon. Just before she raised the limb she'd snatched in her hand, he slapped her across the face. Stars swam in her eyes, and pain exploded in her temple.

She closed her eyes as the world turned black.

Chapter Eighteen

Howard Hodges paced the ground beside Satan's Falls. Back and forth, back and forth in front of Elsie's body. But the voice in his head wouldn't be quiet. He jammed his hands over his ears, trying to drown out the incessant chatter but the trill of her commands echoed in his head, making his temples hurt and the skin beside his eyes stretch with tension. That brought even more pain, and he turned his head up and howled at the starless night.

"Shut up, Hattie Mae. Shut up and leave me in peace!"

"Tell Elsie about her baby," Hattie Mae whispered. "She has a right to know, Howard. You shouldn't have lied to her before."

He threw his hands toward the sky, cursing her with every ounce of his being. It was bad enough she'd nagged him all his life, then forced him to turn into a recluse, to give up the girls and his life, but now she'd been haunting him from the grave.

He imagined her decaying in the ground, pointing a bony finger at him, and he wanted to kill her all over again.

Elsie Timmons would have to do.

He studied her unconscious form, the way her robe had opened to reveal the curve of a creamy breast, her slender thighs, her parted legs and wanted to bury himself inside her one time before she died.

Then he'd throw her in Satan's Falls and watch the devil suck her soul down to the mossy depths of the icy water. It was so crystal clear he'd be able to see her body lying on the floor, see her eyes wide-open in death.

And then he'd be free.

Free from hiding out. Free of Hattie Mae's spirit. Free of Elsie and his past forever.

If only he could free himself of the scars. But that bitch Elsie had ruined him for life.

Now it was her turn to pay.

ELSIE FINALLY SUMMONED the courage to open her eyes. Water from the falls crashed over the rocks only a few feet away.

She'd listened to Hodges ranting and was frightened. She shuddered, weak and numb from the cold, and blood loss. Her ankle throbbed relentlessly. Lightning lit the sky, splintering the darkness, and she thought she saw the shadow of a hawk soaring above.

Deke. Was he on his way? Maybe following the falcon. She was so disoriented she was almost hallucinating. Maybe he was the bird….

Hodges touched her bare skin, and she shivered in horror.

"That's it, little Elsie. Wake up now. We have lots to do before you die."

She had to stall. "I heard you talking to Hattie Mae."

Rage tightened his jaw. "She won't leave me alone. Haunts me all the damn time."

"Maybe she's your conscience," Elsie said, grasping.

"Hogwash," he said crossly. "But she wants me to tell you something."

His finger brushed her jaw, and she barely resisted the urge to strike out. But if she convinced him to talk about Hattie Mae, maybe she'd learn if he killed any more girls. And maybe Deke would find her by then. If she fought now, he might push her over the cliff. "What does Hattie Mae want you to tell me?"

His nasty chuckle reverberated in her ears. "That your baby is still alive."

Elsie gasped. He was even more cruel than she'd imagined. "You are truly evil," she hissed.

"What?" He pretended to cower, but he was laughing at her. "You don't believe me?"

"No," she said. "I saw my daughter's grave."

"That doesn't mean there's a body in it," he said in a singsongy voice. "We only dug a grave so you wouldn't ask questions."

Her heart pounded. Was he lying now just to torment her, or could he be telling the truth? Was it possible…?

"Too bad you'll never get to see her." He unbelted the robe at her waist and cold air assaulted her as he looked down at her body. "But at least when you die, you'll know she's in a happy home. Not that she'll ever know anything about you…."

DEKE'S STOMACH CLENCHED when he caught sight of Elsie lying on the ground, Hodges perched above her. Hodges gripped a gun in one hand, the other one on Elsie's robe. Bile rose in his throat, and he motioned to Thurman to move to the left and create a diversion. Seconds later, the brush on the left side of Hodges rattled. As if the animals in the forest heard his call, a loud roar that sounded familiar, like the werecat or lion that had saved him and Elsie earlier, pierced the night. Hodges shifted slightly, then stood over Elsie waving his gun toward the direction of the sound.

Deke leaped forward through the clearing and pounced on Hodges from the rear, knocking his weapon to the ground with one whack to the man's wrist. All the pent-up anger and rage he'd felt toward Hodges since he'd heard Elsie's story exploded inside him, and he unleashed it, pounding the man with his fists, slamming his head against the hard-packed ground repeatedly. He wanted to kill him. To make him suffer.

"You will never hurt Elsie or anyone else again," he growled.

Hodges hissed, scratching and kicking, but Deke was part animal himself. He felt an incessant urge to tear apart his prey, piece by piece, limb by limb. He'd leave nothing but bare bone for the other animals to feast on.

Hodges kicked him in the shin, and they rolled several times until they lay at the edge of the cliff overlooking the waterfalls. Deke shoved him closer, until his head dangled over the precipice. Hodges deserved to be thrown into the pit and left to rot.

But Elsie's voice brought him back to reality. "Don't, Deke. Let him go to jail."

Thurman gripped his arm. "Come on, Deke, let me handcuff him. Go take care of the woman."

The woman?

His woman. Elsie. She was all that mattered.

Reality weaved its way through his irrational need for revenge. Hodges could rot in jail. Death was too quick and easy.

He dragged the sick bastard to his feet, then

shoved him toward Thurman. The agent hand-cuffed him while Deke raced to Elsie. She was shaking and cold, fumbling to tie her robe closed. He gritted his teeth and tied it for her.

Blood stained the ice below her foot. He cupped her face in his hands. "Are you all right?"

Her teeth chattered. "I am, now that you're here."

He jerked off his coat and wrapped it around her shoulders, then examined her wound. The bullet had missed the bone around her ankle but hit the surrounding tissue. He tore off his shirt and T-shirt and tied the T-shirt around the wound, then jerked his shirt back on and lifted her in his arms.

Hodges cursed and shouted, making empty threats, his words almost incoherent. Thurman shoved Hodges toward the path that led to his car, then into the backseat.

Deke followed, hugging Elsie to him, grateful she was alive. Although part of him still wanted to kill Hodges….

THE NEXT TWENTY-FOUR HOURS passed in a blur. Elsie relayed Hodges's declaration that her baby was alive, and Deke promised to check it out. She wanted to be there when he dug up the grave, but he insisted on taking her to the hospital first. Thankfully, the bullet hadn't lodged too deeply, and they removed it and bandaged her foot. They'd also cleaned up the scratches on her body, treated her for frostbite and forced her into bed to rest because she'd suffered a slight concussion.

The medication and head injury made her woozy and weak. But as she drifted to sleep, she thought of Deke. He had been quiet on the ride to the hospital, almost withdrawn. He was probably thinking about ending the case and going back to Colorado and his family. Was there any place for her in his life?

When she woke up two hours later, Deke sat at the foot of her bed, an odd expression on his face. Not a smile. And he didn't move to touch her.

"Elsie, I did as you asked."

Oh, God…her baby. "And?"

He cleared his throat, then glanced down at his hands where he gripped them. Although they looked clean, dirt particles were embedded beneath his nails. He had dug up the grave, partly with his bare hands.

"It's okay, just tell me the truth, Deke." She inhaled for courage, glad he'd spared her the ordeal of watching. She couldn't have stood seeing the tiny grave open, and her baby's bones inside.

He squeezed her hand. "The grave was empty."

Relief poured through her, as well as anger toward Hodges, Hattie Mae and that social worker. "I told them I wanted to keep my baby," she whispered, tears flowing down her face. "I told them and they took her anyway." Her voice broke. "How could they have been so cruel to make me believe she died?"

Deke shook his head as if he couldn't understand the cruelty, either. "Hodges will face charges of kidnapping along with murder."

"I don't know what to do now," she said honestly.

Deke stroked her cheek. "I'll help you look for your daughter if you want."

She tugged the sheet around her, a million questions racing through her head. Should she track down her child and let her know that she loved her? What if her daughter wanted nothing to do with her? What if she uprooted her happy life? What if she wasn't happy, what if the family she'd been given to hadn't been good to her?

Elsie had to know the truth.

She couldn't have her daughter go through life thinking her birth mother hadn't wanted her, that she'd abandoned her, that she was unloved. Not the way Elsie had.

But it wouldn't be fair to Deke to drag him into another mess.

"I need some time alone, to think," she whispered.

DEKE HEARD THE WORDS and tensed. She needed time alone. Just as she'd said in her note to him. He'd tried to make himself believe that Hodges had forced her to write that goodbye letter, but the words had been hers.

"You've done so much for me already, Deke. I can't ask you for anything more."

He hesitated, a sharp pain stabbing his heart. Elsie had no idea what digging up that grave had done to him. He'd been a wreck himself, praying the baby was still alive. He hadn't wanted to come back and relay more bad news. But the fact that Hodges had robbed her of her own child for all these years had nearly driven him crazy with anger. His hands shook now just thinking about the injustice. And wondering where her little girl was... How could Elsie stand the deception? And now the uncertainty...

"I want to take you back to see Deanna," he said in a gruff voice. "That is, unless you're still hellbent on opening that center at the manor first."

She shuddered. "I'm glad Hodges is in jail," Elsie said softly. "And that we know the truth. But I think it's time to put the past behind me."

Except for the little girl...he knew she couldn't let that go. And neither could he. "What about the teen center?"

"I still intend to build a teen center, but not there, not with all the sordid history. The children, they don't need to have the legacy of death, the ghosts around them. The scent of bodies in the wall."

"I think you're right."

"I'm ready to move forward now," she said. "To meet my mother." A look of courage lit her face. He'd never known a woman as brave as Elsie.

"I'll make plane reservations for tomorrow."

She twisted the sheet edge in her fingers, not looking at him, then nodded.

He stood, wanting to fold her in his arms so badly he had to grip them by his side. But she had to make the first move. "I'll let you get some rest, then pick you up in the morning and drive you to the manor to pack."

She nodded, looking anywhere but at him, and he sucked back the urge to beg her to stay with him. But Elsie had to make her own choices. If she didn't love him or trust him by now, she never would. He took one last look at her, then closed the door.

When he escorted her back to Deanna's, he'd have to say goodbye.

THE NEXT MORNING, tension vibrated between Elsie and Deke as he drove her back to the orphanage. She wanted to throw her arms around him and plead with him to talk to her, to love her, but something had changed between them.

Maybe the fact that her child was alive had bothered him. Maybe he'd only made love to her out of pity....

Whatever the reason, he was going to leave her, just like everyone else in her life.

"Sorry I'm late," he said as he'd helped her into the car. "But we found Thompson. He was at the airport."

"Have you talked to him?"

"We interrogated him this morning. Apparently Hodges killed Sheriff Bush, and he tried to kill you. He left the bloody animal and warning. But Thompson ran us off the road and shot at us." Deke hesitated. "He also shoved you into the street." Deke paused, folding his hands together. "Thompson claims he and Dr. Mires got caught up in Hodges's business by accident, then they didn't know how to get out."

So, when Hodges hadn't been tormenting her in the manor, Thompson had followed her in town. They had both wanted her dead. "I imagine he profited from the adoptions."

"Oh, yeah." Deke kept his eyes glued to the road while she studied the debris left by the storm. Muddy snowbanks, broken twigs and limbs lay everywhere, the remnants a reminder of the shattered parts of her life.

"What about Renee Leberman?"

"Thompson killed her."

Elsie sighed. "But Hodges killed the doctor because he was going to reveal that he was still alive."

"Did you ask Thompson about my baby?"

"He claims he doesn't know what happened to her," Deke said. "Hodges must have handled that on his own."

Disappointment sliced through the little bit of hope Elsie had held on to overnight.

Silence fell between them, the tension thick and unnerving. A few minutes later, he handed her a pair of crutches, helped her into the house and upstairs so she could pack.

"I have to free the falcon before we go," Deke said.

His gaze met hers and locked, and for a moment she read some undefinable emotion, but he turned and fled down the steps before she could speak. She threw together a suitcase, then moved to the window and studied him as he brought the injured bird outside. The falcon rested on his forearm, its head tilted slightly as Deke spoke to it. She imagined Deke's soft voice, that silent connection he shared with the animal, then watched him lift his arm skyward.

For a moment, Deke and the falcon's profiles blended, and the shadows of their silhouettes melded in the early-morning light. The two were one—man and animal, animal and man.

The bird took off in flight, soaring upward, peaceful, at home in the sky.

Deke deserved, needed, that freedom just as the falcon did.

And if she pursued her daughter, no telling what she might find or how long it would take. After all she'd put Deke through, she couldn't tie him down any longer with her problems.

She had always stood alone, taken care of herself. She would face her mother, then decide what to do about her child. And God help her, she'd let Deke return to his own home, free and carefree like the birds of prey he loved so much.

DEKE CLOSED HIS EYES on the plane and tried to rest, but sleeping was impossible, not knowing what he had to face.

Telling Elsie goodbye.

Setting the falcon free had been easy. Setting Elsie free would be the hardest thing he'd ever done in his life.

Exhausted from her ordeal with Hodges and the injuries she'd sustained, she slept the entire flight. He ached to brush her cheek with his hand, to pull her into his arms and hug her, to know that when she returned home, she would want to be a part of his life. But that would never happen.

Something was off with him. He was too dark. Intense. He was all or nothing. No wonder a woman couldn't love him.

She finally awakened when the plane landed. "It's not too far from here to your mother's," he said.

Her eyes widened, the familiar fear lingering, but she nodded and gathered her purse. God, he loved her courage.

He assisted her off the plane, commandeered a wheelchair to assist her to baggage claim, then rented a car to drive to Tin City. His Range Rover had been totaled, but it was replaceable.

Not like Elsie.

She remained silent the entire ride, staring out at the scenery. The mountains and snow looked similar to Tennessee, yet her home here was nothing like the one in Wildcat Manor.

Finally, he drove up the mountain toward Falcon Ridge, then turned to go to Elsie's mother's house nearby. She checked her face and hair in her compact, but he reached out and closed it.

"You look fine, Elsie."

"Maybe I should have waited until the bruises faded. Until I could walk without crutches—"

"Your mother is desperate to see you."

"She knows I'm coming?"

"I called and told Rex this morning."

She gave him a faint smile, then he walked her to the door, his heart squeezing when he saw the joyous smile on Deanna's face as she opened the door. Seconds later, she pulled Elsie into her arms and the two women wept as they hugged.

"Thank you for bringing my baby home," Deanna whispered.

He nodded, squeezed Elsie's hand, then looked into her tearstained eyes. The glow on her face would be freeze-framed in his memory forever. Then Deanna coaxed Elsie inside, fussing over her as if she were still four. Deke slowly drifted away from the door, leaving the two women the privacy they deserved for their long-awaited reunion.

ELSIE PAUSED when she stepped inside the doorway, her head a blur of broken memories, scents and images. She had finally come home now, had found her mother, and everything Deke had said was true. Somehow, just by looking into Deanna's eyes, she knew that her mother loved her, that nothing she could confess would break their special bond. That she had hurt her mother by not coming home sooner.

"Come on, dear, you look exhausted." Deanna helped her to the sofa, then spread an afghan over her legs. "Let me fetch us some tea." She hesitated. "Oh, dear, we've missed so much. Do you even like tea?"

"Tea would be great," Elsie said with a laugh. "But don't be gone long, Mom. I want to just sit and be with you."

Deanna burst into tears, and Elsie laughed, battling her own as the woman rushed to the kitchen.

The room grew quiet, and she glanced out the window to see Deke driving away.

He'd done his job. Fulfilled his promise.

Now she had to let him go.

Grief welled inside her, and more tears filled her eyes. She had everything she needed for the moment.

Everything but her little girl.

And the man she loved.

The three of them could be a family. No, she couldn't entertain storybook fantasies.

Deanna bustled back into the room with the tea, placed it on the tray, then handed Elsie a small box. Elsie opened it and her heart swelled at the sight of the charm bracelet her mother had given her when she was little.

"I saved it all these years, hoping you'd come back," Deanna whispered.

Elsie traced her finger lovingly over the memento, then hugged Deanna again. Even without her child and Deke, her cup runneth over.

Chapter Nineteen

Almost a month had passed since Deke had left Elsie at Deanna's. She and her mother had bonded beyond anything she'd ever imagined. Elsie had finally confessed about her past and how Deke had found her, and Deanna had listened, cried and hugged her while they both relived the nightmare of their separation.

But time was healing them, bringing them closer, the dark memories and nightmares finally abating. She'd even taken a step in finding her daughter, and had signed onto the national registry, in case her daughter ever wanted to search for her. She'd also asked Deke's brother, Rex, to suggest an agent to work the investigation, and he'd promised that he'd farm her case out to someone reliable.

But each day Elsie ached for Deke's return. She'd reunited with Hailey and met both of Deke's brothers. They had been quiet about Deke, and she assumed they knew what had happened between them. Hailey claimed that Deke liked to take off alone at times, cementing her feelings that she'd made the right choice by letting him go.

But she hadn't realized how much his absence would hurt her, how much she'd miss him.

Maybe he was happy. She could only hope.

Deanna parked the car at the Falcon house, and she braced herself for the family Christmas celebrations. She hoped Deke might be present, just so she could see him one more time. Take another mental photograph for her memory book.

Inside, Hailey and Rex's new house smelled of cinnamon apples, cider, hot chocolate and baked goods. Christmas decorations abounded, and twinkling lights lit the outside of the lovely new Victorian house. The traditions were foreign to Elsie, but she loved them. The families hugged and shared holiday greetings. Rex and Brack looked positively handsome, but disappointment fell when she realized Deke hadn't come home.

Although a cheery mood floated through the room, the next hour passed in agony for her. She wanted the day to be over, wanted to go home and cry her heart out.

Deanna squeezed her hand, and she pasted on a happy face. It was her first Christmas with her mother and she couldn't ruin it. They had just passed out the eggnog when the front door opened. Snow fluttered to the floor, and suddenly Deke stood in the entrance, his cheeks flushed, his hair dotted with moisture. Her breath froze. He looked magnificent.

His gaze caught Elsie's and a dark, mischievous look glinted in his eyes. Suddenly tension rippled through the air, and Elsie noticed Hailey, Rex and Deanna exchanging odd looks.

Deke moved toward her, his expression serious. "I have a Christmas present for you, Elsie."

Uncertainty reared its head, along with hope. She started to speak, but he pressed a finger to her lips. "I think you'll like the surprise."

Elsie slanted a look at the Falcons, at Hailey and her mother. Anticipation lit their eyes.

He reached behind him and opened the door. "They've come a long way," Deke said. Suddenly, a little girl bustled inside, brushing snow from her coat. Elsie recognized her immediately. Renee's daughter with the big eyes. "Allison?"

Her grandmother tottered in behind her, wearing a tentative smile.

"Elsie, this is your daughter." Deke threw his arm out in a wide arc, then bowed as if he was introducing royalty.

The little girl smiled uncertainly, then played along with Deke and curtsied.

Elsie stared in shock. "My daughter?"

"It's true," he said in a gruff voice. "Allison is yours." He gave her a secretive smile, then whispered, "Renee found out she was terminally ill and went to Thompson in search of you. She was going to contact you to see if you wanted Allison."

"You're sure?"

"I checked through social services and found copies of Renee's private files."

But Thompson had killed Renee before she'd called Elsie. Tears blinded her. This beautiful little girl was her very own daughter. The baby she thought had died.

And Deke had brought her home.

Allison took a step forward. "My other mommy died, but Mr. Deke said you're my birth mommy. Is that true?"

"Yes, I've missed you so much." She knelt, then took the child in her arms. Behind her, clapping, laughter and shouts erupted. When she glanced up, Deanna was hugging Allison's grandmother and Hailey was crying.

She picked Allison up and held her close to her heart. She never wanted to let her go. "Thank you, Deke."

He nodded but a sadness also weighed in his expression. Elsie desperately wanted to talk to him but someone mentioned presents, champagne and Santa Claus and the festivities began.

TWO HOURS LATER, Deke stepped into the backyard for air. Elsie was happy. She had her daughter and her mother. That was all she needed.

But he needed more. He wanted to be a part of her family, wanted her to be a part of his. But that damn note still held him back. He had smothered her. He had to be patient. Give her space.

Damn it, being patient was killing him. He wanted her more than he wanted life itself. His job, the birds, meant nothing now without Elsie in his life.

Deke's hand fell to the ring in his pocket. He was being foolish. Selfish even. He'd just given Elsie her daughter, and now he wanted something back.

But not out of gratitude. God, no.

Out of love.

But what if she said no? He was still so intense. With him, it was all or nothing.

"I love you, Elsie. Will you marry me?"

He'd practiced the words so many times that he didn't realize he'd said them out loud until a gasp echoed behind him. Damn, even his senses were off. Normally he would have heard someone come outside. He smelled her sweet perfume before he turned around.

Elsie bit down on her lip. "You're not asking me this because you think Allison and I need protection?"

Deke whirled around and grabbed Elsie's arm. She had to realize his proposal was sincere, even if he hadn't known she'd been listening. "This has nothing to do with protection, although hell, yes, I do feel protective of you, but that's because I love you, Elsie." His voice cracked. "I would do anything in the world for you. Don't you understand that?"

"You already have given me everything, Deke. My sanity. An end to my past. You've freed my conscience, given me back my soul." Her voice thickened with emotions. "And now you gave me my mother and my little girl. I can never repay you for that."

Deke ground his teeth together. "Love is not about repaying or keeping score. I don't want your gratitude, Elsie. If you don't love me, then I can accept that."

Elsie moved her hand to his cheek, and he shuddered.

"How can I not love you, Deke? You're the most wonderful man I've ever known. You're gentle and kind and you've stood beside me through everything. You didn't even judge me when I told you about my baby."

"But you said I smothered you, that you needed to be away from me—"

Elsie's chest squeezed at the anguish in his harshly spoken words. She felt as if she was dying inside. She couldn't watch this big strong loving man suffer, or let him lay his heart on the line again and not confess the truth.

"Deke, I said that to protect you." This time she cupped his face with her hands. His eyes glimmered with hurt. Pain that she had put there. Because she'd felt compelled to stand on her own. And because she'd been scared. "Hodges told me that if I didn't get you off his back, that he'd kill me, then come after you. Writing that note was the only way I knew to make you leave. I…" Her voice broke. "I love you so much I couldn't stand the thought of him hurting you because of me."

"But they were your words, Elsie. Somewhere deep inside, you didn't trust me to save you, to stand beside you. What is love without trust?"

"I know I'm a mess, Deke, a coward. My relationship with my daughter is new and tentative, and you're a falconer, a loner at heart. I was afraid, but I also thought you wanted your freedom, that it wasn't fair to tie you down."

His jaw tightened, the heat radiating from his

body speaking of desire, hunger, a need that she felt in her own chest. "What isn't fair is for us not to be together. Don't you see, Elsie? I used to think I needed to be alone, but that's not true anymore, not since I met you." His voice cracked. "Some falcons mate for life. And when we were together, when I made love to you, I knew that I belonged to you and you belonged to me. Forever."

"We do belong together, Deke. I believe that now." Her voice wobbled. "Maybe I was scared that if I told you how much I love you, how much I need you, that you'd leave me like everyone else."

A war of emotions flickered in his eyes, before he finally relaxed. Then he dragged her close to him, his breath brushing her neck. "Say it again, Elsie."

"Say what? That I wanted to save your life, that my life didn't matter if you weren't in it anymore—"

He swallowed, his voice gruff when he spoke, "Say that you love me."

A smile tugged at the corners of his rugged mouth, and Elsie's heart fluttered with renewed hope. "I love you, Deke. I think I have from the beginning. And I always will love you."

His voice grew more commanding, "Now say you'll be my wife."

She traced her finger along his mouth. "I'll be your wife."

He lowered his head and kissed her, raking his

hands up and down her back, his body quaking with the intensity of his kiss. "Listen to me, and don't ever forget this. I will never abandon you, Elsie. Never. Not for a million years. Not as long as there are forests and trees and animals and land."

A giggle sounded behind them, and they both paused. Allison leaned around the corner, hugging the new teddy bear Renee's mother had given her beneath one arm. The charm bracelet from Deanna glittered on the other. "Are you two getting married?"

Deke wrapped his arm around Elsie's shoulder, not bothering to hide his affection. "Yes, ma'am, we are."

Elsie nodded, sliding her arm around his waist. He didn't have to worry about her running again. She was his now and she always would be.

Elsie smiled at her daughter. "Honey, we don't have to rush—"

"Speak for yourself," Deke growled into her ear.

The little girl skipped toward them and smiled up at Deke. "You don't have to wait on account of me."

"No?" Deke asked.

"No, but I have a question."

Elsie brushed a strand of hair behind one ear, still hesitant, still afraid to push too hard, but still in awe that Deke had found her little girl. "What is it, Allison?"

"Is Mr. Deke going to be my daddy?"

Elsie glanced at Deke, waiting on a reply.

"Yes," he said, squeezing Elsie's hand then reaching for Allison's. "The three of us are going to be a family."

Allison's mouth quirked sideways, the tilt to her chin a replica of Elsie's. "Three?"

"Well, five," Elsie said with a smile. "Grandma Leberman, and Grandma Timmons are our family, too."

The little girl wrapped her arms around their legs, and they embraced her, hugging her close. "Goodie. I always wanted a mommy and a daddy, and two grandmas."

Deke leaned over and swung her up on his hip. "You actually have another grandmother and a grandfather. Mom and Pop Falcon."

"And Aunt Hailey and Uncle Rex and Uncle Brack," Elsie added.

"Wow." Allison's eyes lit up. "Just one more question?"

"What is it, sweetie?" Elsie asked.

"Mr. Deke, will you teach me how to talk to the birds?"

Deke brushed a kiss on Allison's cheek. "Of course, any time you want, pumpkin."

Tears dampened Elsie's eyes as she hugged her daughter to her side, then leaned over to kiss her husband-to-be. Deke was the man who had given her everything, the love and family she'd always wanted.

The future they would share together with her daughter.

And maybe one day, a baby of their own, a little boy who could continue the falconer's legend.

* * * * *

*Don't miss Rita Herron's next book
of romantic suspense,
LAST KISS GOODBYE,
on sale in August 2006,
only from HQN Books!*

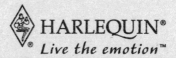

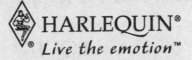

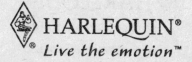

Harlequin Historicals®
Historical Romantic Adventure!

*From rugged lawmen and
valiant knights to defiant heiresses
and spirited frontierswomen,
Harlequin Historicals will
capture your imagination with
their dramatic scope, passion
and adventure.*

*Harlequin Historicals . . .
they're too good to miss!*